The Heart Island Anomaly

Brian Neil Roy

www.brianneilroy.com

All rights reserved.
ISBN: 1534705708
ISBN-13: 978-1534705708

Written by Brian Neil Roy
Edited by Jeanne Marie Leach, Marléna Lynn Bartlett
Artwork by Juan Carlos Barquet © 2016.
Author Photo by Jess Godnai

DEDICATION

To Pat and Jack. With only **one** life to live, they gave me theirs.

CONTENTS

ACKNOWLEDGMENTS

I wish to thank several people who have contributed to this novel in many ways.

For Jeanne's patience and lessons. For Jess and her creativity. To the Brevick family for their love and support. For 'Steph-erly' precision and for Marléna's countless hours of editing, creativity, support, and love. To all my beta-readers and fans. I love you all with everything I have.

CHAPTER 1

He brought himself to his knees. The blazing sun reflected harshly off the water and white sand surrounded him. Averting his eyes from the glare, he focused downward at his tattered tan pants. He was covered in wet sand.

Where am I? Kneeling on the beach, he listened to the waves crash, trying to conjure memories, as the odor of salt filled his nostrils. He raised his hand to shade his eyes from the sun's reflection, and a sudden jolt of pain shot up his right arm. He quickly covered his injured limb with his left hand and winced, rocking back and forth.

A vile stench of fish wafted past him and he pursed his lips. Convulsing and trying desperately to hold back from vomiting, he doubled over. The smell passed and after a few deep breaths, the feeling subsided. His body shook as he made his way to his feet, swaying as he tried to gain some balance. He gasped at the sight before him, and with his body limp, he fell forward to the ground with a thud.

As he lay unconscious, she came to him.

"Wake up," the woman pleaded as she leaned over the injured man.

He opened his eyes and rolled over in the soggy sand to face the source of the voice.

She floated backward. Darkness shielded her face. She spoke to him in ethereal rhythms and melodies that flooded his brain and sounded muffled and unclear.

"What's happening? Where am I?" he questioned, trying to gain clarity.

"You are back and you are sleeping. You need to wake up," the woman commanded with urgency. She stood and her dark robe straightened as she hovered above the beach.

"What do you mean I am back? Who am I?"

Shadows covered her hooded head and glimmers of blonde hair shined through, and she disappeared from the dream.

Waves covered his body as the tide rolled in and splashed him awake. Immediately the pain resumed at the previous intensity. He rolled over and up to his knees to view the sun setting over the horizon. Sand and spit sprayed as he coughed out a mouthful of the sea. His lips were chapped and his tongue felt swollen. Raising an arm to wipe his mouth, he shook with jolts of pain surging through his extremities.

A dozen tiny red dots pricked the side of his wrist, and the rest of the outside of his arm was covered in a large red welt. Something had bitten him. As the waves sloshed past his body, the cool salty waters eased the sting. With a deep breath in preparation, he made his way to his feet, taking in the view of the sea.

The sun had passed the horizon, and as a faint golden color glimmered across the waves, the sky melted into a blood-orange hue. Mesmerizing waves of blue spheres spanned across the water as if it was a wrinkled polka dot dress.

"What are the odds of getting stung by a jellyfish anyway?" he wondered. "One hundred percent." He laughed at his luck. "One hundred percent."

As he looked away from the setting sun to the west, he gaped at the sight before him. Dozens of boats had washed up, all destroyed. It looked as if the gods grabbed an entire harbor, crumpled it up, and sprinkled the boats across the shore. For a slight moment the pain subsided, replaced with wonder, and he tried to comprehend what had happened on this beach. His heart beat wildly in his chest as he took in all the destruction and the realization hit him.

I'm trapped, aren't I?

Sweat broke the surface of his skin and he unwillingly

began to breathe heavily. Which boat was his? His thoughts wandered desperately to find his craft, some supplies, his identity, or even something to drink. He shook his head as he scanned all of the wreckage in the distance. There was not a single ship that hadn't been covered in barnacles.

Turning inland to the jungle was the only possibility of fresh water. Tremors shook his exhausted legs as he stepped to the edge of the vast leaves and vines. Pushing some plants to the side, he huffed at the struggle. With leaves, sticks, and vines aside, more obstacles were exposed. The jungle was too thick and intertwined to get in. Taking a few steps backward, he looked down the edge of the jungle to see if there was an alternative entrance or path. Tensing his lips and stomping his foot, he let out a growl knowing he would need a blade to get through this mess.

Littered amongst the sand, the contents of the sea crafts gathered along the edges of tidal pools all the way to where the jungle met the beach. The tide was coming in fast and was nearly to the edge of the jungle. From his position, he couldn't see down the beach to the end in either direction. Was he on an island or the mainland? *This must be a secluded island, or there would be a lot of people looking at this incredible sight.*

Stepping into the warm water before him, he waded out to his hips to get a better look down the beach, but something stopped him. Jellyfish were all around him blocking his path to a better view. He looked over his shoulder and back-peddled to the shoreline to safety.

Corroded by the elements and overtaken by barnacles, various items on the shoreline sparked his interest with their possible uses. He found several jars filled with different substances displayed as if they were used for scientific purposes. He moved quickly through the sand and glanced across the beach in search of something he could use to cut some vines or trees. He uncovered dolls, boxes, jewelry, ammunition, crab traps, and many strange items he didn't recognize.

"Thank the gods!" he let out as he dove to the ground. A scabbard protruded from the sand. This sheath probably housed a fine sword, he gave it a yank and the pain in his arm screamed, but the blade didn't budge. He straddled the blade with his feet, bent over, and grabbed it with both of his hands. Leaning back, he let out a grunt, using all the strength in his thighs, and released it from its resting place as he stumbled backward. With a thud he landed butt-first to the ground and latched on to his hurt arm, dropping the sword.

The leather rain-guard that separated the cross guard from the base of the blade was weathered and stiff. Made to keep moisture from getting into the scabbard, this seal fused the blade in tight. He tugged at the hilt, but he couldn't get it free.

"If only I had a blade to score the leather to free this sword. The gods do have a sense of humor," he mumbled at the irony. Risking the possibility of breaking the hilt off the sword, he closed his eyes as he smacked it down against the rocks. It worked. Drawing the blade, he admired the craftsmanship. It must be a fine blade if someone also took the time to craft a scabbard. He let out a deep breath, and his nerves calmed a bit now that he had the comfort of a weapon and the means to get into the jungle.

Though the beach was deserted, the island itself wasn't without a variety of sounds. He jumped and tossed his head in the direction of each noise in the distance. Thoughts of crazy natives crossed his mind. For all he knew, he was exploring in some sacred place where his presence would anger the island's inhabitants. Looking over the sand for recent human presence, he found nothing; no foot prints, no garbage, only these destroyed ships and their contents trapped in tidal pools.

If there were intelligent beings around here, then this place would have been looted dry. *Unless this is all junk*? He raised a theatrical fist, shaking it at the gods. Then ceasing his outburst, he frowned, remembering his amnesia. Was there anything he had accomplished worthy enough to merit rewards greater than junk? He imagined opportunity was only deserved by the worthy and he pretended to apologize to the sky.

To add to the theory of his isolation, sealed trunks and boxes were completely weathered which suggested no one had been there for a long time. Anyone with a sliver of curiosity would have opened them. Whatever phenomenon was at play certainly had been active for some time without human interaction.

"What a treasure!" he yelled out as he placed his hands on his hips and puffed out his chest. This place in its entirety was his, and he declared himself king. Cheering for his luck, he paused to look at his wounded hand. The score of his fortune versus the wilderness was even.

The light barely poked above the horizon and he realized his time was nearly up to look for fresh water. He needed to build a shelter. He needed a safe place to rest, away from the elements.

Off the edge of the shoreline, he found a large, broken container. The box wasn't big enough to create a shelter with, but it did contain various tools. On the bottom shelf, he found some dry wood and a perfect board to create a campfire.

As he rested the board on a flat rock, he placed some

dry grass at the end of a shaft in the wood and rubbed a dowel in fast repetition across the groove in the board. After a while, the faint glow of an ember shined at the end of the board. Quickly and carefully, he fueled the fire by slightly blowing on it and dropped the fresh ember in the small pile of grasses. It lit with ease, and he fed the fire fresh air by wafting his tired hands about. As the flames built strength, he concentrated on the crackles of the fire which produced familiar melodies.

With a few twigs and dried leaves, he fed the fire a few moments longer to ensure it would remain strong while he explored for more fuel. Standing, he brushed off the wet sand from his legs and grabbed his short sword. At the edge of the jungle, he chopped and slashed, clearing a few feet at a time. He bundled plenty of dead vines and large dried-out leaves and brought them down to rest by the fire. With one final trip, he returned with some larger branches, gradually stoked up the fire with some longer-lasting fuel, and enjoyed the warmth for a few minutes.

A large branch protruded from his newly carved-out section of the jungle, long and thick enough for the main support of a shelter. He laid down the sword and grabbed the tree with both hands. Leaning backward with all his weight, the branch broke free from its hold. He dragged the beam toward the opening he'd carved in the side of the jungle. Angling it up, he placed it against the base of a large stump. For this basic debris shelter, he chopped and leaned sticks against the main beam and pushed them into the ground. Then he lashed the tops of the sticks leaning against the beam with some split vines. He adorned the outside of the shelter by covering it with leaves, moss, and ferns found on the jungle floor.

Sitting back, he admired the craftsmanship and believed his construction would hold through the night. He completed the makeshift shelter by lining the floor inside with a bed of leaves he had harvested while clearing the bush. After adding more fuel to the fire, he stretched out his sore muscles and let out a hearty yawn. With the opening facing the base of the fire, he carefully entered his creation with caution and laid down.

Licking his lips proved useless for his swollen tongue. His mouth was now completely dry. Swallowing hard, the predicament invaded his brief accomplishments and positive attitude. *Who cares where I am or who I am for now? I just need water, otherwise, it's not going to make any difference. I'm going to die.* Closing his eyes, he tried to get comfortable, but now the fire felt excessively warm. No matter the position, a rock or a branch bore into his back. Despite his uncomfortableness, his mind calmed as he realized there was nothing he could do now, and he started to drift off.

Half asleep, a strange, high-pitched noise entered his mind. Foggy and in a dreamlike state, he focused on the sound to determine what it was. Each second it came clearer until he realized the source. It was a boar. He opened his eyes to see the beast frantically squealing and charging toward him. His first instinct was to scoot further into the shelter, but as he turned, he realized his temporary home was encased in fire.

CHAPTER 2

Australia: Four weeks earlier. . .

"Sweetheart, wake up," Janice called to Alexa as she opened the door to her daughter's bedroom and poked her head in, grinning.

"Just a little more sleep, Mom," Alexa begged from under the covers.

"Well, I wouldn't want you to miss your birthday, dear. I guess I'll have to put away this gift then," Janice playfully prodded.

Her daughter sat up quickly with her crazy blonde hair in disarray.

Janice shook her head and smirked. "Okay close

your eyes, sweetie."

"Come on, Mom, I'm too old for surprises." Alexa covered her crystal-blue eyes but peeked through her fingers.

"Oh, excuse me! Seventeen-years-old! We should be careful of your old heart," Janice scoffed, then scooted over and placed the present on the bed and sat next to Alexa.

Alexa delicately peeled back the tape off the present, careful to not tear the wrapping.

Janice couldn't help but roll her eyes and sigh as she reached in and tore the paper off the top of the package.

"Mom, you know I like to save the paper!" Alexa scolded, giving her a light tap, shooing her hand away.

"Well, you can use this as your eighteenth birthday present as well, considering how long it's taking you to open it." Janice burst out laughing.

Alexa smiled back and dove into tearing off the paper and opened the box with force. She tilted the box, and a second wrapped present fell into her hand.

"Cute, Mom, how many boxes deep this time?"

Janice motioned for her to continue.

Alexa wasted no time unraveling her mother's joke. Two boxes in, Alexa produced a silver necklace and gasped at the sight, knowing what it was.

"I figured it was time to pass it on. You do remember the story, sweetheart?" Janice asked and received an approving nod from Alexa.

The young woman sat upright, eager for her mother to tell her the tale of love once more.

"A long time ago, there was a scientist, the brightest of her kind. She had the highest degrees in physics, engineering, computer science, and more—all by the age of eighteen. With a grant from the world consortium, she was placed on a project to recreate the earth. As the chosen seeding humans orbited the planet in the great Galactic Refuge, she devised the first terraforming network.

"Each device was placed strategically around the planet, forming a network of fission and fusion devices that deconstructed and reconstructed materials. The network shared basic subatomic resources, sending them through channels so they could be used to recreate the mountains, rivers, plains, and all the facets of life before the human destruction. The project was a success, except for a small hiccup. Certain places on the planet refused to cooperate in the deconstruction phase. Some anomalies were not accounted for.

"Entering into this story was a pilot, deft and handsome. The two met briefly in meetings covering the reconnaissance mission. She and he, as colleagues, explained the plan to the soldiers—a delicate plan to fly in and take some samples from the two island chains causing the disruption. As she described the organization and apparatuses needed for the mission, she couldn't keep her eyes off the attractive captain. He had trouble concentrating as well, with this amazing heart and mind, merely feet away from him. Obviously, there was a connection between the two.

"As time went on, they continued with mock missions and adjusting the equipment to reduce the risk of this critical opportunity. Their blushes turned to love with each encounter. He would steal her away from the lab on occasion to share special moments under the stars in the training pods.

"Finally, the day came when the crew left the orbit for the surface of the planet. The man and the woman met once more in the loading bay where they confessed their undying love for each other and kissed one final time before the departure. She set the terraformed network on pause and placed her hand on the window of the mothership as they neared the atmosphere. The transport ship hovered alongside and the mission captain boarded and the door sealed shut behind him. He turned, staring at his love, and placed his hand on the glass of the door of the transport ship.

"Both the man and the woman felt something was wrong, and she fell to her knees and sobbed. With a command from the admiral, the captain turned the transport ship, and it blasted toward the anomaly. The ship glowed with a fiery blaze as it pushed through the atmosphere. That was the last time anyone saw the crew.

"In the loading bay after their last kiss, he gave her something. This necklace. This promise. It signifies forever. It means undying love. She never married, for she longed for her love until her ashes were passed across the galaxy in memory of the savior of earth. Nine months after the crew disappeared, she bore his child.

I am giving this to you because your father and I have found the greatest love that life will ever offer. May this token bless you, as it has blessed our bloodline for generations."

Alexa passed the necklace to her mother and pulled her hair to the side.

Janice clasped it around her neck, and they both hugged deeply as tears welled in both their eyes as the legacy was passed on.

"Now, let's make some muffins for dad. He'll be home shortly, my dear," Janice said with a wink as she wiped the tears of joy from her daughter's eyes.

They expected John around noon, and they shared smiles while thinking of him as they prepared for his arrival. More often lately, he had been sent to train at the base, preparing troops for their engagements in the South Pacific. A gleam in Alexa's eyes shined as her thoughts went to her father. She was excited to see him.

"Oven, set oven temperature to 450 degrees Fahrenheit," Alexa called out as she looked up from her console and sent commands to the oven. She scurried around the kitchen gathering a mixing bowl, measuring cups, a beater, and baking tins. Arms full, she worked from left to right and laid out each device in the order they would be used. *Mise en place* is something Alexa was firm on practicing. She believed in always making sure everything necessary was accounted for before any action took place, a trait inherited from both her mother and father.

"Let me wash my hands, sweetheart." Janice

paused and said, "You do realize I love you, right?" Janice leaned over to Alexa to place a kiss on her cheek.

"Um, yes, Mom. I love you too. Are you making fun of me?" Alexa stuck her cheek toward her mother for the smooch and pouted, pretending to be hurt.

"No, I think it is cute how you are always so prepared. And you know, the important things in life are never mentioned enough. I wanted to let you know that I will always be with you."

"Planning on going somewhere I don't know of?" Alexa wondered, raising her eyebrow.

"No, silly. Like I said, I will always be around," Janice answered with a smirk and poked Alexa playfully in the belly.

Alexa let out a hissing sound as she sucked in her belly as if it popped.

"Just like your dad," Janice chuckled and stepped over to the sink to wash her hands.

§§§

Alexa's cheeks reddened from the special attention. Looking over the island of kitchen utensils, she grinned and watched how graceful her mother was. Not a single wasted movement. All of her friends at school reminded her of how attractive her mother was, and while it certainly made her feel uncomfortable at times, they were right and she knew it. The light from the kitchen window caught the highlights in Janice's long blonde hair. She turned to Alexa as she wiped her hands and moved a strand of hair out of her face, exposing her freckles.

"Mom, you look radiant today, I must say," Alexa said, smiling.

A wave of nostalgia washed over her as she thought of the love between her parents. Alexa glowed while watching her mother. Maybe someday she would know that kind of love. Janice was always so thoughtful, always showing John and Alexa how much she cared for them.

Her friends were surprised that her parents were

still together. Every one of their parents were divorced. Alexa imagined that people either never found the patience, or weren't willing to expend effort in their relationships.

True love starts with a spark and continues forever with some elbow grease, Janice would always say. Alexa believed her mother was right, and by watching her, anyone would know how Janice applied her own teachings. Alexa always saw her mother welcome John with love.

Time and time again, Alexa witnessed her father returning showers of compliments to Janice. Alexa thought of how charismatic and gentle her father was, sweeping Janice off her feet every time their eyes met. When together, it seemed as if they were transported to a different world where only they existed, where everything else was background noise.

"We need flour, baking soda, and salt," Alexa called to her mother, reminding her of the task at hand.

"Ouch!" Janice called out as she lifted the flour from the shelf. She shook her hand and placed her finger in her mouth to calm the sharp pain. A moment later, she pulled her finger out and inspected it. A single drop of blood formed at the tip. Movement on the shelf changed her attention. The flower bag hit the floor and a poof of white powder shot out. She lifted her wrist and mumbled *"emergency"* as she stumbled and knocked the bowls and beaters off the shelf.

Their eyes met in terror for a split second as Janice fell forward and bounced off the floor.

Alexa sprinted and crouched over her mother.

"Mom, what's wrong? What happened?" Alexa screamed as she turned her mother over, supporting her head. Janice dazed and in and out of consciousness, trying to speak, but nothing came out.

Alexa grabbed the communicator and yelled, "Emergency!" Looking down to her mother, Alexa saw a distant blank stare in her eyes. Janice was fading fast. "Mom! Mom, please stay with me! Look at me! Please don't go. I love you! Don't go!"

Janice turned her head one last time and mouthed a single word to her daughter. *Love.*

Within moments, the emergency crew arrived. They assessed Janice's condition and saw the wound on her finger.

"Snake!" one of them said. "It must still be here in this room. They cautiously searched and finally cornered the brown snake, identifying it as venomous.

Thrashing and bawling, Alexa screamed for her mother as the men pulled Janice from her arms. She flailed her arms and legs, trying to get loose from them as they forced her down to the ground. Something suddenly stung her arm. She looked over and saw a needle emerge as one of the workers pulled it out. Waves of reality slowly pulsed out of view as consciousness left her.

§§§

John arrived to witness the EMTs filling the back of the trauma craft with a hover stretcher. He shot out of his government-issued Jeep and ran to the patient bay to see the body bag. His heart beat heavily in his throat as he tried to rip the bay door open, but the medical examiner pulled him back. Panting and screaming, he fell backward, tangling himself with the man. The doctor pulled a needle from his belt, but John knocked it in the dirt and struck the man in the chin. The man fell backward, knocked out. Puffs of dust rose around him.

As John turned to the vehicle's door once more, he caught a glimpse of his daughter on the porch. She was laying on the deck next to the bannister.

"Alexa!" he hollered as he pushed through two more medical crew members who were attempting to restrain him. As she raised her head groggily, John saw her tear-soaked cheeks.

The agony of loss crippled him and he collapsed in front of his daughter. *Janice is gone!* Gasping for air, he struggled to refrain from screaming and wrapped his arms around Alexa. Rocking back and forth, he embraced his semi-conscious daughter. No words came to him to soothe his daughter. The love of his life was just torn from his grasp.

Hours passed as John rocked Alexa in his arms on the porch. They sat in silence, holding on to what was left in their shattered world.

"John," The voice of his best friend, George, woke them from the hours of silence.

"When did you get here?" John could barely think straight and was still holding his daughter.

George held out his hand and lifted John to his feet. Alexa stirred and her dad helped the girl sit up, and placed a kiss on her forehead.

George led John and Alexa in the house. Alexa sat at the table, and George motioned John toward the coffee machine and placed a cup underneath. Quietly George said, "It's important you take her away from this house for now. She will heal better outside of her element. You still need to go on your trip." He leaned in with a small smile as he placed his hand on his best friend's shoulder. "Janice would have wanted you both to go on the cruise."

John looked at his daughter and saw the pain in her eyes. He looked at George and he returned a nod. George was right, as usual.

CHAPTER 3

A low murmur emanated from the trees on the northern side of the island. Cretus, weakened from the last storm, sat on his throne. He could feel them coming. He could sense the proximity of the necklace. He could smell their blood. He had been waiting for this for nearly a thousand years.

With a click in his voice, he called to his minions.

Seconds later, three blackened beings with their heads down floated into the chamber. Clothed in long jute robes, masking their red eyes with hoods, they surrounded him.

"I can feel the necklace; the bloodline of my brother is close!" Cretus shook, raising his hands. "There is a ship entering the outskirts of the island chain. It is further than you have reached before. Bring the ship in." Cretus commanded, in a deep resonating voice, echoing off the cavern walls. Bubbles of red liquid metal from the depths of the land threw shadows across his throne. He raised his hand and the beings vacated the room to start their task.

A storm was coming.

Deep within the bowels of the caverns, Cretus looked across the room at a skeleton, outstretched and weak, on a raised stone slab next to a blackened pool. His brother. Cretus laughed at the possibility to finally finish him.

Murmurs from afar increased in volume as the charred, blackened beings could be heard chanting louder and louder, summoning a deep storm off the shoreline.

"You are too weak, brother," the skeleton hissed from the stone slab. Cretus knew his brother was right. This was the opportunity of a lifetime, but he may have failed already.

"Still to this day you doubt me as you lay there,

weakened under my hand. You're barely alive, and you can't stop me," Cretus roared.

"My son will stop you. He knows how to find you. He knows your weaknesses." The skeleton sneered.

"Brother, there are so many things you don't know. I won't waste my time with the details, but suffice to say, he knows nothing of the sort," Cretus said, his laughter reflecting off the blackened walls of the cavern. He floated over to the blackened pool below the stone slab. Cretus leaned over the skeleton of his brother and screamed. "I will kill the girl and the father! I will kill your sad excuse of a son! He will die!"

Echoes from the outburst shook to the core of the island. At the southernmost tip, the skeleton's son was slowly burning alive.

CHAPTER 4

Embers from the campfire floated to the dry leaves at the entrance of the shelter. Suddenly, the flame leaped to the leaves and grasses surrounding him. His butt to the ground, he scampered backward as he tried to gain traction in the sand. A gust of wind swept in, forcing thick, hot smoke and sand to smother his face and enter his lungs. His foot slipped and kicked out a support beam. The shelter crashed down. The main beam cracked under the intense heat and caved in.

The weight pinned his leg to the ground. Panting, screaming, and thrashing, he tried to free his leg. Scorching hot vines and sticks burned into him. His skin on his chest down to his legs bubbled and curled. He couldn't get free.

The pain exceeded his threshold. He gave in and closed his eyes and passed out in defeat. As he fluttered into unconsciousness, the boar slammed into the support beam, and it rolled off him.

He awoke surrounded by ash. The sun breached the horizon, sending bright yellows along the beach. Surprised he didn't go up in flames, he sat up quickly, thinking he was on fire, and found the fort had been destroyed by the massive blaze. The sudden movement stirred up some soot, and he coughed a bit. As he waved away the smoke and inspected the fire's remains, the charred palms circled around his body, resembling a black snake. Pretending to tip an invisible hat, he acknowledged the coal serpent for protecting his life throughout the night. Where was the boar? He'd like to express his gratitude to the animal for saving his life.

Standing, he inspected his torched clothes. The shirt, now threadbare, barely clung to his body and was nearly taken off by a slight passing breeze. Blowing in the wind, his shorts, which at one time were pants, had nearly disintegrated. The entire beltline served as fuel for last night's fire and provided no dedication to assisting in covering his personal business.

He inspected the burns on his belly and legs and couldn't believe his eyes. Tight, pink skin pulled toward the center of the wounds, and scabs had already formed, showing amazing progress in the hours he slept. He touched his skin, expecting to scream out in pain, but the pain never came. Impossible! How long had he been asleep? How many sunrises had he missed?

At closer inspection, tears came to his eyes and he dropped to his knees. Thin lines of scar tissue traced his body. His fingers followed over the remnants of wounds in an attempt to ask them how they happened. Hundreds of scars.

"What has happened to me? Who am I?" he muttered, his dry voice scratchy as the tears drenched his face. "This is just too much to handle; I don't want to know. I really don't want to know. I just want some water."

A cool morning breeze swept along the shore, chilling him and pulling him from his thoughts. Goosebumps sent a chill through his body. With his pants around his ankles and his arms wrapped around his waist tightly, he decided to clothe himself was the best decision. He turned to the wreckage of ships for some possibilities.

Along the shoreline, he counted at least twenty distinct vessels lining the beach, by identifying the individual hulls alone. Large sections of ships were crushed, torn and strewn about the land in a massive display, suggesting the intense power of devastation. The variety of boats and other unfamiliar crafts amazed and confused him. He couldn't recall anything resembling some of them. A few ships were far more weathered than others, dating their introduction to this land further into the past. His brain melted over the idea. He only was familiar with the ships that had been here for a considerable amount of time. Hairs rose on the back of his neck. Breathing hard, his thoughts raced, and sweat arose across his brow. Thoughts of who and where he was paled compared to this. *When am*

1?

He approached the first boat slowly with an outstretched hand, carefully feeling the ship built far beyond his years. As his fingers met with the ship's surface, he struggled to understand its reality. Had he slept for years, decades, or centuries? Had these objects crossed time to exist in his world? Nothing around him gave any clues to determine the current year.

Halfway to being completely consumed by the land, the sailboat he touched measured fifty feet in length. It had a weathered, gray wooden exterior and a large hole in the hull. With seaweed protruding out of the opening, it appeared as if tried to vomit out the sea's unwelcoming intrusion. He peered inside the hole to find sand had filled the entire space, so he moved on to the next boat for more clues and treasures.

He walked around the hull of the sailboat and sloshed through a tidal pool to inspect the next ship which appeared to be a large, steel, storage ship. The hull remained intact. He knocked his fist against it and listened to its metallic resonance. The material confused him. He didn't know of any type of sea craft ever composed entirely of such an element. How could it possibly float? Intrigued by what it could contain, he hopped up to reach the top half of the ladder that had broken in two and climbed onto the deck to explore the storage spaces onboard. He opened the door to the main compartment to find it spacious and fully intact, housing several large containers.

The large wooden containers towered over his head and were at least four-feet wide and deep. Each box remained completely sealed and tied with metal strips welded shut. Pulling with all his might, his muscles tightened as he tested his strength on a strap and realized he would need a tool to open it. He cursed and shook his fist at the crate as he backed his way out the storage area and continued off the ship down the broken ladder. At the last rung, he let go and thudded into the cold sand, bending his knees to handle the impact.

Brushing off the sand from his bare bottom and legs, he moved on to the next ship, which was cut in half, leaving a huge hole at the starboard side. Placing his hands on either side of the opening, he poked his head in and looked to his right, up the compartment toward the bow and then back, facing the stern. As he entered the boat, a wave rolled in and sloshed past his feet. The majority of the space inside the ship was living quarters, including a small kitchen and three beds. He looked in the cabinets at his feet, which were all open. The doors were mostly broken off due to the tide rolling in and out of the ship. He could see where the definitive line of water damage stopped nearly at his hip level. He realized anything below this line would most likely be destroyed by the ocean as it ripped through the vessel every few hours. Looking up at the cabinets above the bedding area on the port side, he found a machete and a fishing knife.

Suddenly the ship filled with water from a larger-than-normal wave. He was thrust backward and braced himself by dropping the machete and grasping on to a cabinet door. A canister with a funnel-shaped red top fell from the cabinet and onto the counter, belting out a deafening tone. He jumped back, banging his head on the ceiling, and fell to his butt. Reaching out a hand, he gracefully caught the canister as it rolled off the counter. The smeared letters on the can made it difficult to decipher its usage. The letter 'A' defined the start of the words displayed, but the rest of the text were left to his imagination. *Annoying Can.*

He clumsily dropped the can as he made his way to his feet. The canister belted it's cry again as it landed perfectly on the button by the horn. Startled again by the noise, it sent him backward, tripping over a cabinet door and back to his butt. Out from the cabinet dropped a dark-blue short- sleeved shirt. He smiled as he grabbed the button-up shirt and felt the soft cotton threads between his fingers. Holding it with outstretch arms, he gave it an approving nod as he read the name embroidered in red. *Rusty.* The word *mechanic* underlined the name in smaller stitching. With a quick sniff, he approved, and the shirt draped perfectly, fitting over his lean frame.

"Now I don't have to find my old name; I guess I'll

be Rusty Mechanic," he said sarcastically. Laughing to himself, he stood and soothed the bump on his head with his hand. With a satisfied grin, he looked down at his bareness and acknowledged he looked pretty silly and chilly.

As water swept through the gap in the ship once more, it splashed up his legs with a cool rush. He jumped through a small opening toward the stern and rummaged through the cupboards in the main cabin.

Let's see if the captain has some clothes. Rusty unlatched a small closet and discovered a solution to his bareness. Rubber-bottom boots and a few pair of pants sparked his excitement as he sat on the soggy bed and put on his new clothes. The tan pants resembled his old pants, except for the fasteners on the sides and on the fly. He worked the contraption on his thigh and realized it exposed a pocket.

Back and forth he glided a strange metal tab that interlocked and released strange looking teeth with a *zzzz* sound. A new understanding filled his mind as he secured his pants. He broke out in a large grin, not for the pants, but because it housed an invention for which he easily found the function. *I like this zzzz thing, better than laces!* The black rubber-bottom boots were a near perfect fit. Rusty tied the laces in a quick knot and stood to admire himself. Humming a new tune, he welcomed a new wave as it sloshed passed him. His feet remained dry and his smile widened.

"Finally, a single success! I have now broken the chain of failure."

Retrieving the fallen machete on his way, he stepped out of the hole in the boat and ventured slowly from the shoreline to the edge of the jungle to the thick undergrowth. His muscles strained, as he hacked and swiped haphazardly at the daunting growth.

Moving some large leaves to the side, he met with the boar head to head. Both were startled and let out a shriek and fled in opposite directions.

Rusty tripped over a vine and fell swiftly to the ground, nearly stabbing himself with the machete. He sat upright and laughed heartily as he realized he probably scared the poor creature far more than he was frightened. Grabbing on to a thick vine, he pulled his way to a standing position and wiped off the dirt from his pants.

A new sound reached his ears. Water. Unlike the steady waves on the shore, this sound was definitely the constant splash of a waterfall. Full of excitement and with a burst of energy, he jumped over and dodged obstacles in the undergrowth until he reached a crystal-green pond. He dipped his hand in to discover the water was warm. His clothes flew through the air as he tossed them, and he jumped into the water. Completely submerged, he gulped, replenishing his dehydrated body. Seconds later, he emerged with a gasp and wiped his eyes.

To his surprise, the waters were clear all the way to the bottom. With a few strokes, he swam to the edge of the waterfall that fed the small pond and showered off the sand from his hair. Small schools of fish rushed away from him, and bits of plants tumbled here and there in the water. The remarkable sight mesmerized Rusty as the sun gleamed into this secluded area. Giant leaves fluttered as a cool breeze swept through the undergrowth. Ferns lined the base of the jungle and grew relatively high to catch the glimpse of the sparse sun rays hidden by the vast leaves above. The spray from the water entering the pond splashed as it met the surface, quenching the area in a peacefully moist mist. He decided he needed to be in close proximity of this pond and intended to construct a shelter close by.

Rusty scrubbed off the sweat, charcoal, dirt, and sand he had gathered since his awakening. With one hand planted on a large, flat rock, he pulled himself out of the pond and lay back to dry for a spell. As the water evaporated from his skin, he inspected his burns and injured hand. To his amazement, they were nearly healed.

He rose hours later in the afternoon to the playful squealing of the boar. The animal rolled around, squeaking in the mud by the shore of the pond. As Rusty watched from the rock, the boar peered back playfully. The black and gray animal was wooly and had two small tusks. It looked rather young and Rusty could see the boar was female.

Rusty decided the boar was not aggressive, and he moved out into the open and headed toward the pond for a drink. The boar watched attentively, half hiding her face in sort of a shy and playful manner. Probably only weighing the same as a bulldog, she looked as if she hadn't hit her maximum size. She scurried playfully in and out of the mud and leaped and rolled around until she decided to venture up a path and disappear for a while.

As he watched her leave, he was surprised he didn't feel hungry anymore. He'd been there for days now with not a single bite to eat. He figured, looking at his body, he still had plenty of weight. If he wanted to, he could follow the boar for a period to see where the animal found food, or he could trap and eat her. He didn't have the heart to kill her, though, considering she did save his life.

"I suppose it would be nice to have a friend, and I shouldn't eat my friends. I have a feeling I could be here awhile."

He decided to travel his way down the path in hopes for some food and to find civilization. Rusty gathered his clothes and boots and sat on the rock to dress. As soon as the last boot was laced, he made a quick trip to the shore to gather his fireboard, machete, and knife. Then he made his way to the edge of the path.

Small amounts of debris covered the three-foot-wide path. The width concerned him a bit, considering the size of the animals using this path. He realized it would support an animal bigger than he would want to deal with. His new friend had left tracks, and Rusty stopped a second to listen for the animal. The sounds of the jungle creatures and insects sang in perfect time, creating a melodic show. He doubted he could hear the boar if he tried. This new adventure and melody sparked energy in his spirit and urged him on. He continued to track the boar's prints along the path, yet he didn't know how far boars travel.

"I could be out here for a while," Rusty stated, realizing the magnitude of the implication. He pushed himself forward quicker. After a few minutes, he rounded the corner to a valley. It opened up to a large mountain far in the distance. To climb it would definitely be a strenuous endeavor.

Upon closer inspection, he noticed several pineapple trees filled the valley. He rushed in, chopped off a ripe fruit, and devoured it, covering his hands and cheeks in a sticky glaze. A thought dawned on him. With his mouth gaped and a chunk of pineapple in his hand, he looked across the grove. They were growing in rows. These pineapple trees were cultivated by some sort of intelligence!

Rusty froze. He scanned the area, his heart beating wildly in his throat. He didn't know who or where he was, and now he had the sudden feeling someone could be watching him. If he was seen taking the pineapple, the owner may not respond kindly, so the decision was simple.

Don't get caught.

Equipped with his machete and knife, he quickly and silently moved back toward the beach, away from the mountain and away from the grove. With a quick thought, he looked over his shoulder and jogged back into the grove to snatch two more pineapples. Rusty removed his shirt, wrapped the fruit, tied the sleeves together and threw it over his shoulder.

A shriek filled Rusty's ears and he turned toward the sound, up the path. The pig rounded the corner and shot passed him in a fury. Protruding from her left hind leg was an arrow. Someone was coming and they were armed.

CHAPTER 5

"Would you like another beverage, John?" the waiter said as he approached.

John stood and stretched his stiff muscles, sore from sitting on a wicker chair. Guests often complained about the uncomfortable chairs.

Towering over the waiter, John stood six feet with a lean, muscular build. The tattoo of the world consortium on his upper arm explained his burly frame. John was a military man. Shaking his head, John held up his hand passing on the offer for a drink. With a nod, the waiter turned to the young woman. She looked as if she was sleeping, and he didn't want to bother her. He nodded back to John and went on his way.

§§§

A slight vibration from his console chirped as it rattled on the glass table beside the chair. Armed with every application necessary for daily life, John, nor anybody else, was separated for too long from their two-inch console.

"Alarm off," he quieted the reminder, checked the time, and placed it back on his wrist. He still had a half hour before the suggested boarding, giving them plenty of leeway.

With flip-flops in hand, he turned toward his sleeping daughter. John tossed the towel over his shoulder and winced. Another command to the console produced a mirror, and he inspected his hair and skin after the time in the sun. A bit of red reflected off of already-tanned skin that he earned during his days outside, training young soldiers. He gritted his teeth as he inspected the sunburn on his arms and chest, knowing that the next shower could be a bit painful. A flick of his fingers here and there subdued his cowlick, and John sent a command to close the mirror app.

He dropped his sandals down and gingerly stepped into them. Alexa, sprawled out on a fully-extended lounge chair, slept with her book upside down on her lap. The silver heart necklace gleamed from her neck, catching his eye and sending John to a distant place in his mind. He thought back to the story of love and how the shape of the pendant resembled the Heart Island.

Janice had worn this same piece since the day they'd met. Crafted from the strongest silver alloy an ancient captain's salary could buy, it had stood the test of time but not without wear. Each nick and scratch defined places in history, tracing memories for hundreds of years. Its existence was passed on to each and every family as a true testament to love and the human spirit, the brilliance of human persistence, and the glory of human kind. But with all its positive attributes, it couldn't comfort John in his loss. The power of the symbol no longer applied to him.

As John stepped up to his daughter, Alexa sat up from her lounge chair. She lifted her hat, exposing her straight blonde hair and petite face adorned with freckles over her nose and cheeks. John's heart ached as he realized she was nearly a mirror image of her mother in her younger days.

She wrinkled her forehead and frowned as she waved her hand in front of his face to bring John back to reality.

The sudden movement in his view woke him from his reverie, and he wiped a tear in his eye, pretending it was sand. "It is time to head back to the ship, sweetie. I bet they have your favorite pasta for dinner. You know, I talked to the captain today and he ensured you would get it." John smiled.

Alexa smiled back, but the emptiness in her eyes shone through and matched his sorrow. She had barely talked since the day Janice died.

"And what would you like to do this evening? Listen to music in the dining area or play a game together?" John put emphasis on the game.

Alexa smirked at his offer as she packed up her

basket with her damp towel. She was exceptional at gaming strategy and tactics, and he cowered inwardly, as he knew he had a challenge on his hands whenever he played against his daughter, regardless of his military training.

He held her hand as they dragged their feet through the damp white sand up the beach toward the loading dock. Tethered to the massive pier, the heavy cruise liner waited patiently for the tide to fill the cove.

With all passengers and crew members aboard, the captain sounded the horn that signified departure was at hand. At the top deck, John and Alexa watched the workers below. From this viewpoint, they appeared to only be comical ants scurrying about as they released the ship from the moorings.

Finally untethered, the ship set sail due east to the fourth island, cutting through the small waves, calm and smooth as ever.

"That's unique," he said as he pointed to colors of the sky. "I think I can see lightning from that tiny cloud."

She looked in the direction he pointed, as they quietly settled at a table for two, and waited for the waiter to take their order.

"Welcome, you two. My name is Andy, and I will be serving you unless you would prefer to just use the console," the waiter suggested with an emphasis on *console*, implying he would rather not wait on them.

John ignored Andy's suggestion, believing the young man was lazy and ordered the old fashioned way. "I will have the fish and chips, and this fine lady with have the mac and cheese, but for now we would like to have dessert first. If it's okay with you, my dear?" John nodded to Alexa, and she added to the order by pointing to the chocolate cake on the trifold brochure resting on the table.

"Good choice," John told her. We will have the cake, a bowl of vanilla ice cream, a large root beer for me, and an iced tea for the lady."

"I will be back in a moment with your drinks and your deserts." The waiter turned and winked cutely at

Alexa.

But Alexa missed the gesture altogether as she stared off into the distance, watching the lonely, colorful storm cloud.

"May I have your attention, please?" The captain's voice came over the loudspeakers. "Due to some inclement weather, we will be adjusting our course to avoid a passing storm. This will be only a minor delay in our schedule, and we should reach our next destination only a few hours later than expected. Please be advised we may experience a bit of rain and some bumps as we pass the storm. The crew thanks you for your understanding and cooperation."

The ship began its slow turn toward the east, attempting to skirt past the little thunderheads.

Andy returned with the desserts and drinks and John thanked him.

"Is it that big of a storm?" John asked.

"I wouldn't imagine so, and usually we don't need

to change course. But don't fear; the captain is a smart gentleman. You're in good hands." The waiter said.

"In this new heading, I think we are going to get wet." John grinned toward his daughter. He realized the small group of colorful clouds were now significantly darker and were growing in size, but he didn't want to alarm her.

"I agree. I don't think we can avoid the storm and it is already starting to rain," Andy said as he placed the pasta and fish on the table and held out his hand as if to catch a drop.

"You want to change tables?" John mouthed to Alexa and she nodded in reply. Then he turned toward Andy. "We would like to move to another table if that's at all possible. Under the covering over there would be the best," John suggested to the waiter.

"I'm sorry, but the covered area in this restaurant is completely full right now. I can bag your dinner up if you would like to eat it elsewhere. I'll also throw in some extras, for the inconvenience. The seating area over there is perfect, and it'll give you a good view of the storm in this heading." The waiter pointed toward the deck chairs under a second enclosure.

"Good idea. It would be great if we could take it to go, and throw in some chips or snacks so we can munch on them later. We'll wait over by the television so we don't get wet." John said.

Maneuvering around the tables, John led Alexa by her hand over to the television, keeping his eyes on the storm in the distance, which was getting closer by the minute. He fidgeted with his console and tried to get details on the storm, but the connection was down. Shrugging his shoulders, he put his arm around his daughter. They both stood in silence, looking through the glass as the ship angled away from the ever-growing thunderheads. Ominous twists and swirls captivated their attention toward the center of the storm, which was now black as night.

As Andy returned with their dinner bagged up, the

first waves hit the side of the boat with tremendous force. Nearly stumbling over the table next to the television, he handed the bags to John.

"May I have your attention, please," the captain said over the intercom. "It looks as if the storm has increased and moved against the weather person's best guess. For the safety of the passengers, please move down to the cabin area and remain in your rooms until further notice. I will offer updates as we progress toward our destination. If you need assistance, please contact a member of the staff by the consoles in your cabin. To repeat, please move to your cabin areas and—"

"It is a category 4 tropical cyclone!" another voice said in the background. "Captain, we won't outrun it!"

"Remain in your rooms until further notice," the captain finished quickly.

In disbelief of what was just heard over the loudspeaker, everyone froze. The moment, however brief, was an acknowledgment to the three thousand passengers and twelve hundred crew members that the storm that just knocked the boat was deadly.

The frozen passengers ramped up to full-blown hysteria in a matter of seconds. They grabbed food. They pushed and shoved their way across the packed restaurant. Tables and chairs knocked over to the ground. The crash of glass plates and cups shattered across the deck. Silverware clanged to the ground, and children's screams filled the air as the people resorted to baser animal instincts.

John and Alexa scanned the room as they crouched under the television set. Alexa pointed to the center of the deck outside the restaurant. With a quick acknowledgment from John, they sprinted together away from the mob. They rested near the center of the ship against the railing far from all entrances and exits, away from the flow of madness.

"Please remain calm," the waiters and staff shouted as they pointed and directed the people to the cabin areas.

"We will wait until the other crazy people have made it down, however fast they would like to," John spoke calmly as his daughter reached out and put her arms around his neck and hugged him tightly. "In the meantime, look at this amazing view," he turned toward the blackness. Rain pelted their faces as they squinted out upon the storm, both knowing it could end their lives.

Each wave rocked the boat as Alexa and John held on, riding the rhythm of the ship. As they patiently waited for the frenzied crowd to disperse, they kept their eyes on their backs. Alexa shook her head as she witnessed a woman snatch a turkey leg from a man who had fallen down.

"What ever happened to humanity?" John shook his head. "The only courteous people are the crewmembers and that's because it was their job. Is it not everyone's job to be courteous?"

"Not everyone had Janice as a mom, I guess." Alexa winked back at him, and they both smiled at the memory of Janice.

A few minutes later, the crazy people had fled

enough for John's liking. He pointed to the wall and drew an imaginary path to the stairwell going down to the cabins. She nodded in agreement and they both moved quickly.

Crouching down, they scooted to the restaurant wall. A huge wave swelled three feet above the deck and it hit, sending them to the ground. Glass shattered, throwing shards across their bodies. John hovered over Alexa, to cover his face and Alexa from the fragments. When the glass stopped flying around, he reached down, grabbed her arm tightly, and pulled her to her feet. Sloshing through the water and debris, they trudged to the opposite wall of the restaurant. Alexa held her hand up to signal for him to wait for the next wave. Seconds later the boat shook as the ocean slammed into the side, tilted the ship, and sent sea water over the top deck.

"Now!" she screamed and they bolted out of the restaurant toward the stairway. Dodging lawn chairs and other wreckage, they made it to the edge of the stairs. A giant wave pushed across the deck, and they both grabbed on to the handrail. Holding on tightly, they dipped their shoulders as the water pushed in around them, nearly dragging them down the stairs. Another wave hit almost immediately.

Something slammed into John's back. It was the waiter. Andy. He was dead. As the boat shifted, the man's limp corpse once again torpedoed through the water directly toward John. As the corpse slammed into his hip, his grip faltered. John lost his footing and fell backward down the stairs. Thumping and crashing downward, he tumbled head over heels, tangled with the dead man's body. With a thud, he cracked his head on the bottom step, knocking himself unconscious.

§§§

Alexa held tight as the ship tilted toward the stern and sent hundreds of gallons of water down the stairs. As she lifted her head, she saw her father being washed down the hallway.

"Dad! No!" she screamed. Half sprinting and half falling down the stairs, she moved with blazing speed as her father was swept away. The first cabin door in the hallway flew open, and a man grabbed Alexa, pulled her into the room, and closed the door.

"Help! My father is out there! Help me!" she screamed as she rushed to the door, but the man blocked it.

"You have to stay here. I can't open the door right now," the man declared.

"No!" Alexa shrieked and grabbed at him. She punched and thrashed out at him.

He blocked her attacks and backhanded her. Falling backward, she hit the ground with a thud.

"Shit, Shit! I'm sorry, I didn't mean to strike you. Stay here and don't open the door till I bang on it! Come on, stand up!" He yelled as he reached out for her.

She pulled back. "Come on, girl, I will get him. Now stand up," he said in a calmer fashion, even though his face was riddled with a frantic look.

Alexa stood and acknowledged his instructions,

mostly to get him away from her. He opened the door, and water rushed in almost up to his hip and took his legs out from under him. The surge knocked him down and he slid into Alexa. He lifted himself back up and yelled back at her to lock the door as he sprinted out of the room. Alexa pushed herself off the floor, quickly closed the door, and locked it behind him.

§§§

Frantic, the man rushed out of the room looking for the young woman's father. Several people were stranded in the hall, battered to unconsciousness or death. As another wave hit, he latched on to the fire hose hanging on the wall to keep his position. The next surge was so hard, the hose released and he slipped down the slick floor. Wrapped up in the hose and coughing up water, he struggled to his feet. Tying the hose around his waist, he grabbed the closest alive man by his feet.

"I hope you are the right guy." He grunted as he trudged through the next wave by dropping his head to the ground. Pushing through the surge of water, he made it past three more doors, when the boat tossed to it side. A huge wave hit it and he slammed into the wall. He yelled out in agony as the hose twisted and broke his arm. Doubled over in pain, he let go of the man and was consumed by the rush of ocean barreling down the corridor.

§§§

Alexa couldn't wait any longer. She opened the door to the wreckage. Most of the restaurant above had washed into the hall. She slammed the door just in time as the next surge of water came coursing down. A few seconds later, she opened it again and sloshed down the hall. The frantic man from the room was wrapped up in the fire hose and had managed to snap his neck. She screamed out at the sight of him. His arm and neck were clearly broken and laid off to the side at awkward angles.

The boat rocked and she lost her footing. The next wave came crashing down the stairs, and she grabbed on to the man's waist for dear life. Seawater sloshed in with such intense velocity that it threatened to pull Alexa off the ragged man. As the wave rushed past her, she held on tight and the force of the wave yanked the pants clean off the corpse. She floated in the momentum of water three-quarters of the length of the hallway. When the surge subsided, she bent over and coughed ocean out of her lungs.

"Alexa!" her father's words were muffled by the rush of the ocean. The boat rocked sideways and flooded the hallway completely as John reached out and grabbed her. She heaved and coughed as he dragged her back up the stairs. The boat rocked back upright, and they slid across the deck and slammed into the railing. John stood and held onto Alexa tightly as he pulled her face toward his.

"Darling, are you okay?" John asked and she nodded "We need to get off this ship now." As they stood, she latched on to her father as another wave grew, rising along the side of the boat, higher and higher. They stood frozen, holding each other in awe.

The sound of a motor pulled their attention to the sky. It was an A class rescue ship. They both looked to the ship with a slight smile which faded as fast as it came. The enormous wave crested far beyond the height of the ship.

Hairs rose on Alexa's neck.

She turned her head to her father. "I love you!"

He looked down at her, smiled with love in his eyes, and kissed her cheek.

The enormous wave came crashing down.

CHAPTER 6

The console beeped on the Admiral's arm, the message urgent. He dismissed the meeting, and as the last person left the room he pinged the sender. He glanced out the bay window of his office. The earth looked beautiful at this angle. The sun slid behind Earth, eclipsing the planet and showing a faint definition of the land. In contrast to the photos of the earth on his walls, the evening was dark. Barely colonized, only a fragment of humans now existed, and it was shown through the sparse man-made lights illuminating here and there.

"Admiral, this is Captain Karin. We have a situation," The voice emanated from the console on his wrist.

"What is it, captain?"

"Cruise ship 22X43B just sent a distress call. They were diverted from a sudden storm. They are nearing the Heart Island anomaly.

"Idiots" he mumbled to himself. "Why are they so close? Is there time?"

"A cyclone drew them in, sir. It is the furthest out we have seen a storm come from the island chain. It is three hundred miles away from Heart Island, sir. I believe we do have time. Should I send rescue?"

"Yes, captain," the admiral said with urgency. "Issue the order for a C class rescue ship and keep me informed. I am on my way." He glanced again at the Earth. The sun began to reappear from the eclipse as a waxing crescent. He squinted, looking for the lights of Australia and then west. A black vortex was visible from space, visible on the surface even in the depths of night. It was huge.

"Captain, send an A class rescue ship. This cyclone is so large I can actually see it."

"Confirmed, Admiral. Strike that C class, send in the big boy!"

With a click, the transmission was cut off and the Admiral set off running down to mission control. He was lean but slow. He just awoke from stasis three months prior and his training regimen was put aside due to the chaos left from the previous admiral. The burning in his chest and legs affirmed his disgust with the previous command.

Sweat broke across his brow and stung in his eyes as he closed in on the last hundred yards to the central command door. Bending over, he breathed heavily. He stood and placed his hand on the scanner and a red light flashed. *Denied,* the text appeared above the scanner.

"Denied? This is my ship! These are all my ships!" He screamed and wiped the moisture from his sweaty hand on his fatigues and tried again. The display ran green and the door slid open. Hunched over, he raised his head and locked eyes with the captain. Wiping the sweat from his brow, he gathered his composure and walked in.

"Status, Captain?"

"Just deployed the big boy. Placing it on the main screen now."

Every person in the room looked to the center screen as the circular vessel left orbit and fired downward toward the cyclone. Measuring only fifteen yards in diameter, it was a single-person rescue pod. In this day and age, the size of the ship didn't matter. It was the tractor beam the admiral was interested in. It could draw in two of these cruise ships, without a doubt. Whether it could handle having a tug of war with a cyclone of this class was to be determined.

"Run the numbers. How close can we come to the chain and how close to the typhoon at these angles?"

"Yes, sir," a voice echoed from behind him. "On the right-hand screen, Admiral."

"Thank you. Explain these calculations."

"The chain's area of influence is strong and the typhoon is pushing the boat toward it. If we come in at a rough, ninety-degree angle, we risk getting pulled in either direction. But we can pull away from above and then over the typhoon. It has a 72% success rate. That is the best we can do."

"And if we send a B class to daisy chain the pull? Hover the B above the A class and have it hold on tight?"

"Calculating, sir." The captain took a moment to engage a couple buttons, then glanced at the screen. "One hundred percent success rate. Good call, Admiral. Should I send the command?"

"Send the command for the B class."

The communication to the launch bay opened and the command was sent. Again, everyone watched the second ship fall from orbit and blaze toward the first.

A beep from his wrist pulled the admiral's attention from the main screen.

"Madam President, I assume you have heard the news." The admiral addressed his wrist console, and stepped into the hallway, away from prying ears.

"Yes, I have and I am not happy. Why are we sending an A class for a cruise ship? That has got to be the most expensive vacation ever."

"We are sending a B class as well, ma'am."

The smirk on her face turned to a scowl. Knowing her temper, he quickly spoke with an urgent whisper into the console.

"Madam President, John and Alexa are aboard. That means the necklace is there."

"Oh, my heavens. Admiral, do whatever is necessary. You have all resources at your disposal. Keep me informed. Do the command center crew members know?"

"No, ma'am, but I am sure they have already calculated the cost of this mission and know someone or something valuable is aboard. I will keep my connection to you open, if you wish."

"Yes, do that," The president said.

The admiral nodded and walked into the room as hysteria broke loose.

"Silence! Status, captain."

"The A class is almost attached, but the storm is now a category five. Average wind speed is 200 miles an hour, sir, and gusts to two-fifty."

"Run the numbers again. And attach the A and B classes first before we tractor the ship. Satellite, zoom to the cruise liner on the main screen."

The satellite's focus left the A class and zoomed in on the ship. The room went silent as the ship came into view, showing two passengers holding on to the railing facing upward towards the A class. The ship was in view one-hundred feet above the liner. One hundred-feet above that was the crest of a wave. Three seconds later, the wave came down over the two ships.

"Captain, the status of the A?"

"Destroyed, Admiral,"

"And what of the B?"

"No chance, sir. The storm and the liner are within the Heart Island anomaly."

"Oh god! No, not Alexa!" A voice from his wrist console rang out, and the Admiral gripped it with his other hand to cover the sound. All the crew in the room turned toward the admiral, and they watched him slowly drop to his knees, shaking his head. The crew now knew what they had just lost.

CHAPTER 7

For a split second, Rusty had to decide. Should he wait for the pig hunters or run? Could they be friendly? His heart raced and beat wildly in his chest. The sound of the trampling feet came closer. With no time left, he darted off the path and quickly covered himself with some leaves. Eventually, he would have to spy on them to judge their intent.

The three hunters came into view. At first, he couldn't believe his eyes. Were they human? Blackened skin, dark as night, shown from under their robes. Two carried bows on their shoulders. As the third being passed his hiding position, the hood flew off its head. The being turned toward Rusty and halted. It looked to be barely over five feet tall, with a flat nose, and larger than normal ears.

Rusty couldn't look away from the being's searing red eyes.

The creature locked onto Rusty's position. Jerking its head upward, it sniffed at the air. Rusty held his breath as hard has he could. His chest burned under the growing pressure. The leaves around him shuffled as he tried to hold back from moving.

With a shrill screech, the being opened his mouth and called out. It turned and ran down the path.

Rusty let out his breath hard and covered his heart with his hands to prevent it from bursting out of his chest.

I need to know what these things are and where they live. I need to stay away from them. Wanting to save the pig that had saved him, he stood with the machete in hand and pineapples still wrapped in his shirt. Rusty followed the being, kicking up dirt in his wake, as he picked up speed.

As he gained on the beings through the twists and turns, he slowed his speed. They were just out of sight and he could hear their rustling on the path. Turning the corner to the waterfall, Rusty lost his footing and hit the ground, sliding out into the open. There they stood. The two with bows drew back with their sights on Rusty. Instinctively, he put his hands up and shielded his face as he gasped for breath.

Suddenly, the clouds opened and rain poured down. Lightning crossed the sky above, and thunder shook the ground beneath him. The three beings jerked their heads to the sky. Fixated on the thunderheads, they seemed mesmerized by the swirl of darkened clouds above.

Rusty watched as they released the tension on their bows and raised their hands above their heads. They seemed to have forgotten him. *Were they praying?* He laid there, unsure of what to do. Slowly, he backed away into the brush. Thrashing their heads back at him, they growled in unison. Step by step, they closed the gap as Rusty remained frozen. They halted ten feet away and pulled back on their bows. Lightning suddenly struck sideways across the sky, and the three beings once again jerked their heads in that direction. Rusty watched as they turned toward the beach and ran.

"I guess they have more important business than killing me." Rusty shook his head in disbelief and saw the boar laying where the men originally stood.

"What was that all about, Maddie?" Rusty yelled over the howling wind, trying a name for the pig, who lifted its head, snorted and laid back down in the mud. "I'm sorry I haven't thought of a better name," he said and stumbled across the opening toward her.

"Oh, and there's no way I'm going to call you that name again. I promise."

The animal snorted as if to say thank you. Slowly, he approached the pig and kneeled down over her. He attempted to distract her while he inspected the arrow still lodged in her back leg.

"So what would you like? How about Sam, Mary, or Margaret?"

The pig snorted and she wiggled her body.

"Okay fine how about Grumpy, or Miss I-Am-Never-Satisfied?"

Again, the boar snorted and looked down and away as if to say his suggestions were foolish.

"You'll be lucky if I can possibly think of one that suits you," he spirited out. "That's it! How about Lucky?"

The pig oinked in agreement. Lucky it was. With a grunt, the pig closed her eyes as Rusty grasped the arrow.

"This is going to hurt, Lucky. I'm sorry."

With a yank, the arrow came loose. A small amount of blood oozed from the pig's leg. She didn't even wince. She was a tough little pig.

"Let's rest that leg, little girl."

After a few pets on her head, Rusty reached down and lifted Lucky. He carried her off the path into the thick of the jungle and laid her down. With a few swipes and slashes with his blade, he gathered some leaves and sticks and constructed a quick leaning shelter. He finished the fort by covering it with wide leaves. Nestled underneath, the pig lay still, breathing evenly as she fell asleep. Rusty carefully stripped a piece of his shirt and wrapped Lucky's wound and laid down next to her.

§§§

A slight sound in the distance wafted to him on the wind. Rhythmic and steady, it increased in volume as it came closer. It matched the pace and timing of Rusty's heartbeat. Far away, it augmented Rusty's rhythm. A chorus of souls rang out as she came into view. He reached out and their hands met as she glided past him. The connection surged through his body and pushed it to the point of ecstasy.

"Rusty are you here? Come to me, my love. Please save me." Her voice entered into his dream, smooth and seductive. She hovered before him. The black robe and blonde hair hid most of her face from Rusty's view. He angled his head to attempt a better glimpse of her angelic face. Something gleamed out from under her hood. Something shiny. Something silver.

§§§

Rusty awoke with his head partially outside the shelter. He sat up and shook from the chill as cool water dripped down his shoulders.

He couldn't shake how real the dream felt to him. "It would be helpful if she could tell me where she was," Rusty said to Lucky in a whisper, careful not to wake her.

Droplets of rain splashed the same places on his face as soon as he wiped them away. He saw no point in trying to avoid getting soaked.

He looked over the wound of the pig as she lay sleeping. The bleeding had stopped and Lucky seemed to be doing well. He trudged out of the shack and back to the open area, which woke the pig. He pursed his lips and mouthed a sorry to the swine as he kneeled over the pond by the waterfall.

"I need some water. I've never felt so wet and dry at the same time."

He knelt by the pond and drank his fill. Standing and wiping his face, he readied himself and quietly snuck up the path to the first pineapple tree. He could see no movement, no blackened men. He scanned the perimeter for tracks, but saw nothing. Satisfied he was alone, he chopped off a fruit and quickly divided the pulp between him and Lucky, who joined him on the path.

"Well, at least I think I've never felt so dry. Now I feel dry, wet, and sticky."

Lucky snorted and trotted back toward the shore and urged him on.

"Hold on a moment. I just woke up." He calmly walked back to the chilly pond to rinse off the stickiness of the fruit, and the sweat from the day before. "If I'm going to meet some people, I must be somewhat presentable, you know," he declared as he splashed water and rubbed the dirt and sweat from his body. Rusty took his time cleaning and appeared back in front of Lucky, refreshed.

"Let's go."

With a small break in the rain clouds, the sun gleamed into his eyes as he exited the path onto the beach. Shading his eyes from the glare, he turned north and looked down the line of boats and vessels. He could see the tracks left by the darkened beings leading away. Machete in hand and companion at his side, Rusty decided it was time to explore this place. Most importantly, he needs to find where the beings lived and potentially how many there were.

He walked over the sand by the line of ships strewn about the shore. Water splashed far off in the distance as the tide receded. Tiny crabs scavenged the sand, and Lucky snacked on them as the two traveled northward.

Rusty gawked at each vessel they passed. The means of construction varied wildly between them.

"When had each of these ships been constructed? Are all the people dead?"

Lucky ignored his questions, digging her nose in the sand to flush out a plump crustacean.

The soggy sand splashed their legs as he trudged

through, keeping the darkened beings' tracks on his right. The northern most point of the land gradually turned east over a long curve.

A large river poured into the land. It almost looked as if a large *V* was cut from the top of this land mass. He couldn't help but think the northern-most portion of this land looked like the top of a heart. Looking down the V to the center of the island, he approached the river. Smoke rose in the distance, spewing high up above large canyon walls. Lucky snorted and kicked up sand at the site and smell of the wood smoke. Rusty was sure it was the hunters and coaxed Lucky to hurry.

"Shall I carry you across?" Rusty asked and Lucky sprinted and splashed into the channel. She was an able swimmer, and Rusty huffed in surprise and followed the swine to the other side. Splashing out of the water, he patted the pig for her accomplishment, and they were on their way across the northern tip of the island. He kept an eye down the gorge, looking for the darkened beings, but they didn't appear.

A slight whistle reached his ears. His heart raced as he looked for its origin. It was coming from above. Screeching from the sky, a huge ball of fire barreled toward the shore. Rusty and Lucky stood in awe at the sight. A black smoke tail mixed with fire streamed in its wake. It was going to hit the shore. He was sure of it.

It smashed into the sand a few hundred feet ahead of them in a thundering blast, throwing yards of sand into the sky. The impact knocked both of the two to the ground. Rusty got to his feet and sprinted toward it. Lucky passed him, snarling and growling at the silver craft, which laid half buried in the sand.

He approached it, his mouth wide open in amazement. As with some of the other ships, it was composed of an unknown material. He raised his hands to his face to shield the heat radiating off the sides. A blast of steam shot around and circled upward, blowing away the smoke and cooling it instantly. Rusty stepped back and wiped the sand and water from his arms and face.

As he turned to the last section of the craft, he saw a

window. The sphere stuck out of the sand, twice as tall as Rusty, and a viewing port was three-quarters of the way to the top of the sphere. Placing his foot on an indent, he pulled himself up to see inside.

With a gasp, he fell backward and thudded into the sand. Lucky nearly jumped two feet in the air, squealing in surprise.

"Sorry, Lucky. It seems that there is someone in there, but she's dead. It scared me."

A loud grumbling down the cavern walls erupted, and Rusty turned and wiped the rain from his brow. They're coming. It's time to go.

As if to match the noise of the approaching beings, thunder rocked the shoreline, and rain bounced harder in the sand. Rusty and Lucky trudged on quickly, rounding the long corner east to south. He looked back one more time at the craft as he stepped out of the line of sight in the jungle. He committed the letters on the top of the craft to memory. *B-Class Rescue.*

Looks like we failed to rescue the rescue crew. He wondered if the ship was meant to help him. A brief sense of comfort came over him at the thought that he could be saved.

The feeling quickly went away as he looked over his scars. Deep lines of pain riddled his skin and his soul. Thoughts of torture entered his mind as he splashed through the puddles on the shoreline. He didn't want to be rescued, to be told he had lost loved ones, to be aware of how his body underwent such a tragedy. There were too many unknowns and he found comfort in his amnesia.

As he rounded the top of the heart, the bend turned toward the south. This confirmed his intuition. It was an island. They had just covered three entire sides. Part of him sank, knowing he was trapped. He would be doomed to live in fear of these beings. Yet he smiled, knowing he could live in peace—never needing to remember the pain and loss of past years.

A half an hour of slow travel brought him to the entrance of a path. At the top right, or eastern side of the heart, he imagined linking with the path by the waterfall. It would make sense to cut a diagonal path to get to the other side.

Both he and Lucky took a short break from the weather at the mouth of the path. Rusty contemplated whether to keep going or just wait out the storm. He was too close to the darkened beings. Rejecting the idea of traveling on the path, he opted to finish circumventing the island.

With a huff, he stood and nodded to Lucky. Both set out into the storm once more. A large structure came into view at the southernmost point of the beach. Closer and closer they trudged through the wind. With each step, the structure grew larger and larger. Within a hundred yards of it, he realized it was one huge stone. An obelisk. He remembered the term. Shaking his head at the gargantuan size, he circled the structure with his hand on his chin.

Just then a tremendous boom echoed off toward the west that shook the ground. He threw his arms out to steady himself.

"Another craft?" he turned to speak to Lucky, but she wasn't there. Looking out to the south he saw her sandy wake as she ran.

"Wait for me!"

Panting and huffing, he trampled on through the gusts of sand and water until he rounded the southernmost tip of the island. The first skeleton of a sailboat near the waterfall came into view. Slowing down suddenly, he dropped to his knees at the sight of craft next to it. It was the largest ship he'd ever seen . . . that is, for as long as his short memory could recall.

CHAPTER 8

The ship towered above the rest of the vessels lining the shore, and Rusty stood in astonishment at the sheer size of the wreckage. Upon closer inspection, it became clear that the back end of the hull was breached, and it sunk deep into the ocean. The ship's bow stood dozens of feet in the air, making it impossible to climb. He considered how he would board it as he scanned the starboard side. At the harsh angle in which the boat lay, the ship's upper deck was level with the ocean, making it accessible about a hundred feet away.

"At least the water is warm enough," he called out to Lucky as he waded up to his waist. Ducking his head under the soft waves, he found a path where he could avoid the jellyfish. A cool wind glided across the waves and fluttered through his hair as he committed himself to the task and dove in. Keeping his head slightly under water and his eyes open, he maneuvered around wreckage and jellyfish to where the deck met the ocean. He grabbed on to the side of the railing and heaved himself up onto the ship, careful not to slide down into the water. He judged his footing and thought over his potential options to search the ship.

He cupped his hands around his mouth. "Hello! Is anyone here?" He waited impatiently for someone to reply, but no one returned his call. With one hand over another, he grasped the cold railing and climbed up the side of the ship's top deck.

On the shore, Lucky paced and oinked at him as he pushed up the steep incline. Rusty held up his hand and waved at the swine, and Lucky pranced, basking in the attention. Smiling at the sight of the playful pig, he turned his effort toward the first covered room. He maneuvered his way over to the entrance. Holding on to the doorway, he focused toward the end of the room. Shattered glass and bottles shined in the morning light, and he hesitated as he glanced down at his bare feet. *This is going to be a challenge.*

He carefully entered the room, hugging the wall, and sparks shot out at him from a strange black apparatus bolted to the wall. Rusty jumped forward in pain and almost lost his footing. Clawing his way along the wall, he carefully found handholds as he made his way to the back of the room. Feet away from a rather large countertop that ran the width of the room, he jumped and latched on to it.

Amid dozens of broken bottles, he found a single shoe wedged between a pole and the wall. *Maybe the owner of this shoe could tell me where we are*, he thought briefly, as he pulled himself along. On the other side of the counter, Rusty was startled to see the grisly sight of a pool of blood with a body was crammed in the corner. The dead man's hand was lodged behind a solid metal box. He was missing a single shoe.

Rusty heard a noise toward the bow of the ship that sounded like shifting furniture and something banging.

"Hello, is there anybody there?" he called out,

listening patiently. No reply came, yet he held out hope that he'd find someone alive. *The woman of my dreams could be here. I must find her.*

Rusty moved out of the room carefully through the rear exit toward the bow. Again, the noise rang out from a hole in the deck thirty paces away. Hand over hand, he pulled himself up the railing, shaking at the strain in his tired arm muscles. As he looked through the opening, he could see stairs leading below. The noise rang out again as he skirted his way to the stairwell.

Halfway down the stairs, he came upon a problem. The bottom half of the staircase was blocked with the remains of furniture and other wreckage washed in from the top deck. He grabbed hold of the railing and carefully led himself down the stairs. It looked as if there were about two meters of tables and chairs to sift through until he could get into the hallway.

He pulled on a table hard, lost his footing, and crashed into the pile of furniture. The mass shifted and dislodged with force down the stairs, with Rusty in tow. He yelled out as he bumped his way down the last few steps and slid into the slick hallway on his side. Quickly, he reached out as he passed the first hallway and grabbed onto a corner of the wall to stop the descent. With a sigh of relief, he stood up carefully and entered the hallway, keeping a firm hold on the railing. This corridor was perpendicular to the stairwell, which lead upstairs to the deck. He rubbed his throbbing hands and arms for a moment to ease his muscles.

Listening for the banging, all he could hear was his heartbeat in his ears as he tried the handle of the first cabin door. It was unlocked. What would he find on the other side? He swallowed hard, and his heartbeat sped up. Mustering up as much courage as he could, he flung the door open. Two bunk beds stood on either side of the room, and the mattresses were knocked off into the center. To his relief, no bodies were underneath.

He let out a long, deep breath and moved toward the closet. A few suitcases and some coats had made it through the storm. He opened the luggage to find clothes of a man and a woman. They seemed odd to him, for they were tailored in a way that was unfamiliar. This ship had been from a place very foreign to him and of a technology he didn't comprehend.

Rusty reminded himself that his objective was to find people, so he left the room and entered the next door in the hallway. This room was slightly darker. It led him closer to the center of the ship, and the light from the main hallway was suppressed. He opened the door to a gruesome sight of a family and shut it quickly. They were dead. Tears sprang into his eyes and he held his hand to his mouth in horror.

He checked all the doors in the side hallway with the same result. From what he gathered, the storm must have tossed the ship so fiercely to break the bodies as he had seen them. Each new set of people looked drastically contorted. *How could anyone survive this?* No one could have lived unless they were strapped down in a room filled with pillows.

The noise rang out again and he jerked his head toward the main hallway. Sliding down the decline on his butt, he followed the sound. *Thump, thump.* At the end of the hall, he sat at the water's edge. The remainder of the hallway slanted downward, completely submerged. The sound was coming from somewhere under the water.

Thump, thump, thump. The water rippled slightly as the sound traveled to the surface.

With three quick breaths, Rusty sucked in as much air as his lungs could take, and he dove in and thrust toward the first cabin door.

Reaching out, he snatched the handle and gave it a yank. The water sucked in quickly as the sea filled the void and pulled Rusty in. The contents of the room were launched into a dangerous swirl. He opened his eyes and he was bashed in the head by a small table. Dazed, he gasped and water filled his lungs. Heaving and choking, he turned to try to find the door again. Furniture and wreckage whirled around him as he kicked off the wall toward the opening. He navigated himself out the door and turned upward to the surface of the water.

Something grabbed his leg and pulled him back.

Instinctively, he tried to push away, but he froze as he met eyes with a woman. She clawed and grabbed at his legs and stomach as she made her way up his body. Each stroke pulled him deeper under the water. They were both out of air and drowning.

Choking and desperate for air, his chest burned as he tried to grasp on to something. His arms stung with exhaustion, and his mind desperately tried to find a handhold to pull himself out.

Suddenly, her hands let go and she floated downward with her eyes locked on Rusty. He looked up. The surface was ten feet away. He reached for her, but she was too far. He was dying. With no time left, he made his choice and pushed upward for air.

He broke the surface and gasped for breath, coughing out water from his lungs as he watched her float away into the depths. With one more deep breath, he turned downward, pushed off, and reached for the woman. Her eyes eerily remained locked on his face as he descended toward her. He grabbed her arm and pulled her limp body to the surface as fast as he could.

Coughing, he pulled her head out of the water. "Come on lady, you are going to make it." Reaching around in back of her, he squeezed her chest in an attempt to rid her of the water filling her lungs. Nothing. He let out a guttural sound and pounded on her back. Nothing. She was gone.

Still hacking and coughing up fluid, he let go of her and pulled himself out of the water back into the slanted hallway. He turned to watch her lifeless body float down into the dark water below with her long blonde hair swirling in the currents as she met her watery grave.

Convulsing, he sobbed in agony. "I killed her!"

CHAPTER 9

The night before…

The wave came crashing down at an angle, turning the entire cruise liner on its side. Alexa and John were thrown from the deck. With his arms around her tightly, they floated in the air away from the ship. They hit the ocean with a huge splash. The impact knocked the wind out of John. Releasing his grip on Alexa, his body convulsed. Kicking his way to the surfaced, he gasped as he tried desperately to breathe.

"Dad!" Alexa yelled out as she surfaced behind him.

Separated by waves, he turned to see her bouncing fifteen feet away. Water splashed over John's head as he tried to remain afloat. He struggled to keep his head above the waves, but it was impossible. His head bobbled below the waterline. John clawed his throat, desperate for air. Reaching out for her, he slipped below the surface.

He kicked as best as he could to remain close the surface. His legs burned as he struggled. The pain was overbearing and no matter how hard he tried, his legs would no longer move. Drifting downward into the blackness, the glow of the ship's lights dissipated. He held his hands above his head, hoping Alexa would be able to locate him.

Just as he closed his eyes, submitting to a fate of a watery grave, she snatched his outstretched hand. Alexa pulled him to the surface and wrapped her arm around her father from behind. With her assistance, John floated on his back with his head in her arms. They bobbed in the waves as debris splashed in the water all around them. Waves crashed over their heads. With a few slow breaths through his nose, John could relax his diaphragm enough to breathe again, and he tapped her arm signaling her to let go of him.

"We need to get away from the projectiles," John

said, as he heaved and pointed away from the ship. They both kicked their way to a comfortable distance and tread water in the huge swells.

"Conserve your energy," he said to Alexa. "Try to float on your back. We can wait here until it's safe to get to a lifeboat."

"Dad, I'm so tired. I can't swim for much longer," Alexa pleaded and coughed up water.

"Okay, let me get you something to float on and then we can get a lifeboat," John said over his shoulder, as he splashed away toward the ship. Up and over the huge swells, he pushed on until he came close to the ship. Lawn chairs and other dangerous projectiles splashed as they were launched from the cruise liner and landed all around him. He reached out and grabbed a suitcase that floated in the waves like a buoy.

Screams from the ship rang out as distraught people flung themselves into the water, and others yelled for their family and friends.

"Alexa!" He called, as he turned. She was nowhere in sight. He paddled with his left arm, the suitcase in tow, dodging debris and projectiles as they came down in front of him.

Silver from her necklace shined in the distance, reflecting lights of the ship. He spotted her and kicked hard, paddling with one arm after her. Up and over the waves, closer and closer, he struggled. Gasping for breath, the pain in his legs and chest cried out as he neared his daughter.

"Alexa, hold on with your arm in the loop and kick toward the ship so we remain close. Relax, we'll get a lifeboat if it's the last thing I do."

Hours passed as they tread water a hundred feet from the ship, holding on to the suitcase. With each wave, more projectiles and humans were ejected off the deck until there was nothing left for the ocean to throw.

John pointed out the people on the second deck deploying lifeboats.

"Dad, I can't swim anymore," Alexa mumbled, with

exhaustion in her voice.

"Okay, take a break. I'll do the work. Hold on and try to relax. Just float and I'll swim us closer." They made it to the side of the ship and called upward, but no one could hear him. He maneuvered the suitcase under one of the life rafts coming down. "There we go, honey. In a few minutes, we'll have a boat and you can stop your workout. Save your energy for when we need to hop aboard, okay?"

Another wave hit the side of the liner and snapped the winch lowering the boat. It hesitated for a second in midair.

"Swim!" John screamed. They furiously tried to get out from under the lifeboat. A few seconds later, the boat came crashing down on its side behind them. He turned and breathed a sigh of relief.

"Man, that was close. Good swimming, love, good swimming." The lifeboat banged into the side of the cruise ship and forced itself upright. John and Alexa swam to the back of the launch to the ladder.

He called out instructions to his daughter to climb in and situated himself in back of her, holding on to the ladder so she couldn't fall backward. Water poured out of her drenched clothes as she grasped the top rung, pulled herself up, and fell into the boat. John quickly followed suit, desperately ascending the ladder as the waves tossed the small craft against the cruise liner.

Alexa lifted her head to the sight of the other passengers. She screamed horrifically at the bloody, contorted mess of corpses aboard their lifeboat. John came in quickly behind her and buried her face in his shoulder. "Don't look, honey. Don't look." The impact of the boat hitting the water had killed the four passengers instantly.

"Don't move!" A man yelled from behind them. He and a group of men were pulling two life rafts together. "This is our boat. Time for you two to go!" the lean man commanded as he stepped aboard the craft beside John. A light shined off the dagger in his hand as he raised it above his head.

"Engine," John whispered to Alexa as he side-stepped and cracked the man in the face. The blade came down in a flurry. Stroke after stroke, John used the rhythm of the waves and dodged and parried the weapon.

"Bobby, kill him!" another much larger man commanded as he boarded the ship. "We don't have all night!"

John turned to the first man called Bobby and jabbed him in the throat which dropped him to his knees. The larger man was immediately on him now.

Bobbing his head to the side, John threw a punch, but the man blocked it.

A return thrust glanced John's chest as he pivoted to the side. John caught the huge man by surprise with a kick to the groin. With a follow-up to the nose, John slammed his fist down to the big man's face. Turning, he kicked Bobby in the shoulder and snatched his blade off the ground.

"Off the boat!" John commanded with fury, as he held the knife to the fallen big man's throat. Bobby rose and backed his way over to the original craft, hands in the air.

The engine rumbled as Alexa pressed the button.

"Cut the line," John hollered.

"Drondor?" a third man questioned, standing near the lines to the boat.

With a blade to his throat, the big man called Drondor replied through gritted teeth, "Do it."

From behind, John pulled Drondor to his feet, keeping the knife to his throat, and commanded him to get off the boat. As he gradually loosened his grip on the man, Drondor stomped down on John's foot, grasped the knife in both his hands, and turned John's hand outward to release the blade. The dagger hit the deck and rang out with a clang, catching Drondor's attention.

John followed up with a crushing left hand to the nose. Staggering backward, the huge man's arms flailed. He quickly crouched and buried his shoulder into Drondor's chest and pushed him overboard.

The man splashed in the water and his screams

turned to gurgles.

John signaled to Alexa and she pulled the throttle.

They sped off and then circled the ship to the other side. John tried his best to stay close to the big ship, but after a few hours, the gas ran out, and they could no longer keep up with the current.

A twister came in and swallowed the cruise ship and then dissipated, leaving nothing but the blackness of night. Alexa buried her face under the emergency silver blanket as the current tossed the little boat away from the larger ship...

Hours after the storm subsided, John held Alexa's shivering body close. The stars were visible once again. He circled around looking in all directions, but there was nothing but calm waves. They were lost at sea.

The father and daughter both fell asleep holding onto each other tightly, bundled up in a silver blanket, soaking wet and cold from the night air.

§§§

"Dad, wake up!" Alexa shook her father. "I see an island!"

John arose to Alexa's call, and sat up inside the lifeboat. It was morning. "Amazing! We must have been right next to the island when the storm hit. Have you seen the cruise liner at all?" John asked and Alexa shook her head. "Well then, we are still in luck, and I bet we'll see some crew and passengers there."

He grabbed the oars and secured them to the sides of the boat. As he sat up, he found several tied up packages in the oar well. Upon closer inspection, he realized it was contraband. *That's why those men wanted the boat.* Alexa's full attention was on the shore, so he lifted some of the packages and threw them over the edge. Alexa noticed and smiled at him questioningly.

"Nothing we need, sweetheart," he replied. "Once we get back to shore, I should give a call out to my commanding officer and get a lift back home. Hopefully by an aircraft, because I am kind of sick of boats," he joked.

"Me too, Dad," Alexa replied with a smile.

John grinned back, thinking how wonderful it was to finally have a conversation with Alexa, no matter how short it was.

They aimed for a large stone structure on the southernmost point of the island. John shuddered inside knowing what it was. An obelisk. He recalled it during several conversations surrounding the two island-chain anomalies. His heart sank as he recalled the islands' pictures taken from satellites. In the shape of a heart, this island was prone to storms. It refused to be terraformed. No one had ever made it off the island. Scientists had no means of explaining the storms and the inability to terraform these chains. As a result, it became a thing of myth and supernatural powers. The Heart Island anomaly.

John looked to Alexa. The necklace gleamed in the sun. It was the same pendant in the story of love. The last artifact of the captain and the scientist. The savior of earth and her love. Chills shot down his spine. John was there, in the same place where the captain disappeared.

After thirty minutes of rowing, he finally got close enough to the shore to jump out and drag the boat in by hand. He pulled it up to shore and lifted Alexa out and over to dry land.

"Let's see if we can find some food and water. I am getting hungry. How does that sound?" John suggested to his daughter.

As they stood on the beach, John viewed the island to the north and south. Nothing. No buildings, no footprints or other human indications were visible, only the two-hundred-foot-tall obelisk.

"What is it?" Alexa said, as she placed her hand on the dark stone and looked up.

"It is called an obelisk. In ancient times it was constructed for unknown reasons. Most thought it was an offering or a way to communicate with the gods."

Which way? John asked himself. *Is there anyone here?* The island was certainly cut off from the Galactic Refuge, but he didn't want to harm his daughter's outlook on the situation.

They had been through enough as of late to dwell on any new bitter circumstances, and it was amazing that they even survived the previous night.

By mid-morning, the sky was clear, with no indication of any harsh weather on the horizon as before. The storm must have passed and they set out to walk counterclockwise around the island. He couldn't help but notice that there were two peaks rising high above the jungle, where the closest was slightly smaller than the one in the distance. John judged that it would take him two or so days to climb it if he could find a clean trail, or several more days if he had to hack his way through the jungle. It may be easier to walk around the island, but that could take more days by rough calculation.

"Let's walk up to the edge of the jungle where the sand is less deep than it is here. It may be easier for us," John suggested, as he took his daughter's hand. Together, they walked up along the edge looking for something. Anything.

"When we approached, I didn't see anything, Dad. Maybe we should paddle around the island."

"That's not a bad idea, but I really am done with boats for now. If we walk for a while, I'm sure we'll find something just off the shore."

Alexa sighed and mumbled to herself, "Doubtful, because there's nothing here."

John heard her but chose to not say anything. What could he say? She's right. The hours passed, and sweat beaded on John's forehead as the sun hit mid-day. They came upon a brook, snaking its way to the water line. John rushed over to the water, knelt in the sand and took a drink. It was fresh water. Both he and Alexa splashed the crisp water over their bodies to cool off their warm skin, and they drank their fill.

They sat back and listened to the sounds of the creatures at the edge of the jungle. A chirp of a bird in the distance was covered by the smooth, intermittent rattle of a series of insects. Alexa distinguished several distinct sounds as she counted them off to her father. A cricket, a parrot, a monkey. With their hopes and bodies rejuvenated, they moved on to find a shady place to rest. A few hundred yards from the stream, a path revealed itself, cutting into the jungle. John and Alexa decided to break a few yards into the path to take refuge from the harsh sun rays of the late afternoon.

§§§

The men spotted an island nearby.

"Come on, row in unison, idiots," Drondor yelled out. "By the time we make it to the island, we'll all be dead. All we're doing is zigzagging around, and we need to find the other lifeboat that has our stash. I am going to kill those two who took it!"

"Aye Aye, Captain," Kenneth said, mocking him.

With a swift thrust, Drondor cracked him in the back of his head. "One more word and you are going overboard, imbecile!" Drondor yelled back at him.

"You're lucky we even pulled you out of the water," Kenneth said under his breath.

"Something funny?" Drondor grabbed Kenneth's

hair from behind him and yanked his head back. He slammed Kenneth in the nose with the butt of the flare gun and threw his head forward again. Drondor's big arms flexed as he yanked Kenneth to his feet from behind. Stunned from the shot to his nose, Kenneth flailed his arms as he lost his balance.

Drondor placed his boot in Kenneth's back and pushed him overboard. With a large splash, he thrashed about, grabbing at the side of the boat. Drondor stomped down on his hand, crushing his fingers. Kenneth let out a scream and immediately grasped his hand, letting go of the boat.

"Are you going to be a good boy and shut up now?" Drondor thundered.

"Yes! Yes! Please let me in." Kenneth panted and choked, struggling to tread water.

Drondor lowered the oar over the side so Kenneth could grab it. "Ah, ah," Drondor taunted the man as he lifted the oar out just of reach. With a quick jab, he slammed the handle of the oar down on the struggling man's head and Kenneth sank into the blue waters below.

"Anyone else have something to say?" Drondor threatened. The reply was silence from the others. "Well then, row, you bastards!"

§§§

There were six men in the boat and now there were five. All the men worked for Jimmie Drondor, doing his dirty deeds, whereas Kenneth was just a crew member of the cruise liner, helping them get their drugs on and off the ship. They had found that barges were more often searched by the law, so they settled on cruise ships as their preferred method of transportation. It was easier to pass through security, considering the employees at the checkpoints were all paid off. Drondor's men also enjoyed playing the part of tourists by taking advantage of the all-inclusive bar and restaurants.

With a swoosh, the lifeboat skidded to the shore right next to another lifeboat.

"Bobby, check that boat," Drondor commanded with a scowl. Bobby hopped off their vessel and up the side of the stationary boat next to them.

"It's definitely the one that had been stolen from us last night," Bobby called to Drondor, while rummaging through the storage areas of the small boat.

"Are my goods still aboard?" Drondor asked.

"Only half of the drugs are here," Bobby called out, with his head still buried below the deck.

"Those thieves will pay with their lives!" Drondor shrieked. His face reddened and sweat broke on his forehead.

"I can kill them," Bobby offered.

"Just tie up the boat!" Drondor ordered. "You three, find the people who were on that boat and bring them back to me, including the missing half of the cargo," Drondor gestured to Sergio, James, and George. "The tracks lead that way, you morons," he spat, pointing north, as the men circled a large stone obelisk. They turned and set out on their way.

"Bobby, when you're finished securing our boat, get the knife, make me a shack to sleep in, get some food, and make a fire pit!"

§§§

"I'm on it," Bobby replied, showing no emotions on the outside, but his blood boiled at the instructions. As a leader, he believed he should run the hunt and make the others pamper Drondor. He knew that any other member of the crew would mess up following commands. They would be as good as dead by the time they came back with the two thieves, knowing Drondor's temper. He knew they would fail.

Bobby despised this older cousin Drondor and secretly thought of thousands of ways to end the overlord's life. Strategically, it wasn't possible. He couldn't kill his cousin, his superior. There ranks in the smuggling business, with Bobby's father at the top.

His father started running drugs from mainland China to the Philippines and expanded nearly to the Americas. He was well respected, but he was also very hard on Bobby. He believed that his son should earn respect as all crew members had. By making it visibly tougher on Bobby, the crew respected his son more. As a result, Bobby became tough and smart. He learned to appease when necessary and use force and persuasion when necessary.

He finished tying down the ship, snagged the knife, and headed back up the shore to the jungle to get to work on a hut for Drondor. It was past midday, and the world allowed him to finish in good time.

"Make that shit comfy. I'll be damned if I have another bad night's sleep with crap poking me in the back," Drondor called out in his typical nasty tone.

"Will do. How about if I pull out some of the seats from the boat so you can lie on those tonight?" Bobby suggested and then bit his tongue. Ending in a choice was always a bad idea with Drondor.

"No way, those seats are too stiff! If I end up tossing and turning, I'll have your head. I don't care who your father is. I…"

Bobby tuned out the rest of the complaining and got to work hacking down some of the larger leaves to provide cover for the make-shift shelter.

He hoped the other men were making progress on the trail of the two thieves, but he had his doubts.

CHAPTER 10

Darkness fell on the island and the tide moved up the beach, erasing the tracks from the two thieves. It had been hours since Sergio, James and George landed on shore. The smugglers were unsure how close they were to the drug thieves.

"Dude, how long are we supposed to walk to find them?" James asked the other two.

"You know if the boss doesn't get what he wants, we're all dead," George replied.

"Since the tracks were erased by the tide, we're screwed," Sergio added.

"And how long do you suppose we have to walk?"

James asked. "It's really dark and I don't think we will see them."

§§§

John heard the pirates coming. From what he could tell by their voices, they were only about a hundred yards away from them. He and Alexa moved closer to the tree line and could see the pirates' silhouettes, single file, against the edge of the jungle. He quickly kneeled down and wiped away the footprints entering the path. Reaching up, he grabbed a vine on the opposite side of the opening and pulled on it, closing the entrance to their hideaway. The plant was taut, and his muscles tightened as he held it silently under the strain.

"This is bullshit," one of them said in a grating tone. "If we find them, the boss will complain because of how long it took us, and if we don't, he'll probably kill Sergio." He laughed.

"Oh? And why me, gringo?" the man called Sergio said. "Is it because he's just looking for an excuse to suppress my manliness? Yeah, it's pure jealousy."

As they passed the half-covered entrance, the three laughed. John's hands trembled as he struggled to hold the tight vine steady and silent. Alexa had covered her eyes, and he could feel her shaking as she crouched behind her father. He couldn't let these filthy men find them; he had to protect his daughter at all cost.

Moments later, the pirates were several paces past the opening, and John eased the vine back to its position and exhaled in relief. He would have to make something more permanent before they came back. As he let go of the vine, it snapped a few meters above him and came crashing down on the jungle floor, rustling leaves along the way.

John quickly picked up a stone, edged his way out of the entrance, and launched it in the men's direction. They shouted something as the stone flew over their heads and into the side of the jungle. They halted, turned, and darted into the brush where it had landed.

Alexa whimpered slightly and John held her tight.

§§§

"It's a snake!" George yelled, and James backed out in a bolt. He tripped, and landed on his butt and scurried backward on his hands and feet.

"Oh, he got you, homes. You are so stupid," Sergio said, busting out in laughter.

"Bite me, Sergio. You know I hate lizards!" James screamed, as he grabbed on to Sergio's arm and yanked him down in the sand. "How would you like it if I scared you with a fist!" He yelled out and socked him in the cheek. The men mock-wrestled around for a moment until they got their laughs out.

"So what do you think we should do, George?" Sergio asked. In tough decisions, he always relied on George because he was the most senior under Bobby.

George put his hand on his chin and pondered the options. "We should turn back and tell him the prints were washed away by the tide, and the waves came all the way to the jungle, giving us no room to walk."

The men agreed to George's suggestion. It would give them no choice but to turn back. No matter their excuse, Drondor was going to be mad, and someone was going to die.

§§§

The men passed the entrance to the path as John held a second vine to close the gap. His arms and shoulders trembled under the strain. This time he waited until they were far in the distance.

Releasing the vine slowly, he moaned under the strain and pulled Alexa's face to his.

"Okay, this is what I want you to do. Take this knife and dig up some of these ferns and plant them at the base of the opening, and then work your way in. I am going to start intertwining some vines and leaves to shut the entrance. Hopefully, they won't recognize it as a trailhead," John said and passed the knife to her.

"Okay," Alexa acknowledged the instructions as she wiped the wetness from her eyes.

"When you're done, take these leaves, and brush off the sand leading out to the beach so there are no footprints. Do it silently, and always listen for them."

Alexa nodded and they went to work. She found some pieces of undergrowth of varying size and planted them around the small opening while John cut off a few more vines from the back and closed the gap. He snuck out the side to inspect his work, careful of the footprints. It looked good. He snuck back in and then told her of the plan.

"From here we are safe, but this is not the best place to hold a defensive position. We need to find a better place and prepare. John fashioned a broom out of some palm and a stick, and as they walked up the path, he covered their tracks.

§§§

The crew wandered back to the camp where Bobby was still diligently working on Drondor's shelter. They decided to get their stories straight. They each agreed that the prints washed away and they continued to follow the beach for a few hours and then doubled back. Sergio agreed to do the talking this time. It was his turn to take the beating. They vowed to protect him in the case of the worst. Venturing to the edge of the jungle, they gathered some sticks and their composure.

"Don't act suspicious, umm, or scared of him. Otherwise, he'll think something's up," Sergio suggested, visibly shaking in his boots.

The other two agreed and they stepped into the light of the fire.

"Besides touching each other, what in God's name took you so long to come back empty- handed?" Drondor yelled as he got to his feet. He charged after Sergio, pulling his knife from his belt.

"We killed them!" he sputtered, as he backed up. "We figured that's what you wanted?" Sergio questioned, diverting from the story the three men had agreed on.

"Where are my packages then?" Drondor grumbled and swiped at Sergio's throat with the blade. With a push to

Sergio's chest, he knocked the man down in the sand. Drondor sat back down near the fire.

"We chased them down and strangled them. It was a few hours up the beach so we didn't drag them back. They didn't have the drugs." Sergio looked away.

"Why did you not bring them back so they could tell us where my merchandise is? What did you do with the bodies?" Drondor spit in the sand at his feet.

None of the three men replied, knowing the story was broken, and they were now trapped in the lie. Someone was going to die—most likely all three of them.

"We'll see tomorrow now, won't we? Now get some rest. It may be your last chance," Drondor snickered.

Sergio walked down to the water's edge, and the men gathered around him not long after. They complained to him of not following the plan. He explained to them he would have died if he hadn't lied. Sergio suggested a plan where they could kill Drondor tomorrow. The idea didn't account for Bobby, so the other two men disagreed. It was certain Bobby would take Drondor's side. Sergio rehashed his plan to consider switching Bobby to their side, or killing him first. Killing Bobby first would be more difficult. Separating him from Drondor would be hard. The men discussed possibilities, but held more for the option of converting him.

"Trying to get your stories straight?" Bobby asked, coming up from behind them.

"No, we're just trying to survive, brother," Sergio told him. "We all know what it's like. No matter what we say, he'll kill us, even if we did everything right." He had to choose his words carefully because Bobby was relative to the boss, and they were not.

Bobby stood there, looking like he was thinking about what Sergio had just said. "I'll try to talk to him. I'll explain to him we need the men for work. He has to stop knocking off someone whenever they piss him off."

Sergio wondered if this was an attempt at soothing the men. "I'm not sure he's a person anyone could convince.

He seems to get off on messing with people more than getting the job done. Is there any other way?" Sergio asked.

Bobby nodded and looked back at Drondor, who was sharpening his knife on a stone by the fire.

"So did you find the people or not?" Bobby asked. "I want to know if I'm standing up for the right people."

"Um, no, we just followed the tracks and the tide came up and washed them away. We followed them for a few—" George dropped to his knees, grasping at his throat. The wooden handle was unmistakably Drondor's blade sticking out of his neck.

"I've still got it," Drondor's voice rang out behind George. "Oh boy, I got it! I would be angry right now, but throwing a dirk as accurate as that is not an easy thing to do, eh Bobby?" Drondor cackled with an evil joy.

George landed head first in the sand like a sack of rocks.

"Bobby, retrieve my knife, would you?" Drondor

commanded.

Bobby leaned over and pulled the dagger out. Blood spirted from George's throat and puddled in the sand around him.

§§§

Trying to hide his fury, Bobby wiped the blood from the blade. Something had to be done and done now. He looked at the other two men, whose mouths gaped open in shock at the atrocity. With his back to Drondor, he made a stabbing motion, and the other men knew the plan. Bobby turned to Drondor and the men grasped their sticks tight. It was time.

Bobby turned the blade handle-out to Drondor. Looking down, he saw that Drondor still grasped the grinding rock in his left hand. He quickly shifted to his right, spun the blade, and thrust it at Drondor's chest.

Drondor moved to the side and the blade caught him in the shoulder. He screamed out in rage and brought the rock around, but Bobby was out of reach.

Sergio stepped in quickly and hit Drondor across the skull with the stick. The boss dropped into the sand with blood squirting profusely from his shoulder. He hunched over, motionless.

Bobby kicked him in the side, hard, but Drondor just laid there.

"He's dead. Oh lord, finally he's dead!" James screamed out as he stood over the bloodied man and jabbed at the wound in his shoulder with his stick.

Drondor pushed the tip of the stick to the side and pulled it toward him, sending James down on top of him. With a quick jerk of his arm, he cracked James in the temple with the rock, killing him instantly.

Bobby kicked Drondor in the head and lunged back in with the dagger to deliver the fatal wound. The knife slipped into Drondor's chest and he froze. It was done.

Drondor's eyes stared back at him seemingly shocked at the killing blow. His eyes closed and his body convulsed rapidly, letting out a horrific shriek. His arms and legs flailed under the body of James. Seconds later, his convulsions slowed down until they stopped, and his eyes opened. Drondor grit his bloody teeth and he locked his gaze on Bobby.

"It's nice to meet you, Bobby," a voice emitted from Drondor's unmoving lips.

"Wha . . . what?" Bobby shook his head at the strange statement.

"The funny thing is, Bobby," Drondor gurgled with blood shooting from his mouth, "you think it is all over, don't you?" Coughing and hacking up sickening amounts of blood, the body of Drondor laid out one more statement. "Well, it is not over, little sapling. After I die is when I come for you, Bobby." The pitch and intensity of his voice rose as he finished. Blood and spit flew from his mouth. "You heard me!"

With a massive thrust, Drondor's body pushed James high into the air. The corpse's arms and legs pinwheeled as the body smashed into Sergio, who tumbled to the ground.

"Now I come for you, little boy!" Drondor's body wailed and fell back into the sand, dead.

Bobby wanted to feel relief. Drondor was dead. *Or was he?*

CHAPTER 11

John and Alexa had stayed up all night. Dawn was breaking.

"Please, Dad, this has to be far enough away. I'm so tired and thirsty."

John stopped and looked at his daughter. Her feet dragged on the path. "I'm not as concerned with the men as I am with the lack of water. If we rest, it'll be that much more time before we're hydrated."

"Please? Just an hour or so. My legs are so weak and my feet are burning," Alexa begged.

He agreed and told her he would carry her off the path so they could rest for a while. She hopped up onto his back. He grabbed her legs and she put her arms around his neck. Stumbling a bit through the undergrowth from weariness and exhaustion, he pushed on until the path was out of sight and hearing distance.

John let her down to rest next to a fallen tree and went to work scouting the vicinity for predators. Flushing out the undergrowth with a stick, he looked for snakes and other dangerous critters. He circled back and laid down some fresh-cut leaves to blanket Alexa. With her covered up, he put his focus on gathering water. Some of the vast leaves held pockets of dew that glistened in the morning light. Carefully, he collected water by pouring the dew from all of the leaves into a single leaf until it was enough to drink.

"Here, sweetheart. Sit up and drink this," John said. He leaned over and funneled the dew into her mouth.

"Dad, did I mention that I love you? You're such a good problem-solver. I can see why you train solders and engineers," Alexa said, wiping the liquid from her chin.

"Well I love you, too. I hope I have prepared those men and women for success. It is important that they respect nature and humans alike. Here drink more," John leaned down and poured more cool liquid for his daughter.

He noticed that tears had welled up in Alexa's eyes.

"What's wrong, sweetheart?"

"I was just thinking of Mom," she said. "The hardest part is sometimes I can't remember her face clearly." Alexa broke down and sobbed as John reached in for a hug to console her.

She gripped him tightly, laid her head on his shoulder, and shook as the obvious pain emerged in floods of tears. "It scared me so much when we were on the ship and you were washed down the hall. I thought I lost you, too."

"You know, sweetheart, I will always be…"

Alexa's face suddenly turned to anger. "Don't say that! Don't ever say that! That is what Mom said and she

died an hour later in my arms!"

"Alexa. I am sorry. I am so sorry. I can't even comprehend what that could feel like. I promise I will not say it. I love you so much." John hugged her tightly and his tears drenched her shoulders.

"Try not to cry out all the dew, Dad." Alexa smirked, letting him know she was okay.

John smiled, wiped his face, and winked at her. "I'll take the first watch, honey, then I will need to rest. We will be safe away from any human out here, but we have no idea what kind of predators there are."

He covered her back up in the leaves to contain her warmth and she closed her eyes.

She fell asleep within seconds. She was clearly exhausted.

He would keep his daughter safe at all costs.

§§§

Alexa lightly snored as John scanned the area for poisonous or hungry predators. Broadening his investigation, he managed to find a few bright purple amethyst deceivers. These mushrooms were not common where he was stationed on the mainland, but he was trained well in survival skills, knowing which mushrooms and plants where edible. Surprisingly, these were usually found in forests, but he was satisfied with his find.

He created a cup by cutting and folding leaves and gathered more dew and stored it under the log where his daughter slept. Peeling bark away from some fallen logs, he managed to secure a few healthy grubs.

John watched the surroundings, sitting comfortably on a branch above Alexa. Rubbing his feet, he winced with each stroke. In the direction of the path, he spotted a coconut tree well-packed with many fruit, ripe for the picking. It was much closer to the path, and far from Alexa, so he decided to wait until she woke to go for the tree.

§§§

Sweat trickled down Alexa's back as the warmth from the day woke her. She let out a short yawn and stretched her back, raising her arms out and pointing her toes. With a slight shake, she smiled and looked up at her father who was starting to doze off where he sat in his perch.

"A moment later and you could have fallen asleep straight to the ground." Alexa remarked, let out a cute laugh, and urged him to come down.

"How was your sleep?" John asked as he carefully scurried down from the branch and lay down on the ground.

"I'm okay, but my legs and back hurt," she stated as she sat up and rubbed her thighs for a moment and then rested her hands on her knees. "Do you think we are going to have to walk a lot today?"

"I think we need to, but for now, I need to rest. I found you some food to eat while I sleep. Do you think you can watch out for people from that perch and make sure I am not bitten by any snakes for a while?"

"Well, um... depends, I guess. What's for breakfast?" She displayed her best sarcastic face.

"Well, we have some mushrooms, some bugs, and if we are quiet, I can get you a coconut. How does that sound?"

"You really found a coconut? I want one right now. Where is it?"

"Over there," he pointed down toward the path. "Want it now, or can you wait till I nap a bit?"

She looked at him with her pouty face and there was nothing he could do. The pouty face never failed her where her father was concerned.

"Okay then, watch your step, and we have to be very quiet and listen for people and watch for snakes."

"Thanks for the tip," Alexa sassed and smacked him on the back.

At the base of the tree John and Alexa looked to the top, sizing up the climb—at least a thirty-five-foot tree. They brought their heads down in unison and looked at each other, Alexa with a smile and John with a much more disturbed wince.

"Come on, old man, where is the positive attitude? Get up there."

His face changed to business as he gripped the knife in his teeth and started the ascent. Most of the dew had dried off which gave some grip on the smooth bark, but not enough to stop him from sliding down every few seconds. He ended up back at the bottom. Discouraged at the failure, he huffed and stepped aside.

No amount of watching the technique videos of agile people had prepared him for such a feat. They always seemed to do it with little effort, and he realized he did not have the correct body type. He offered a chance for Alexa to do it.

She accepted and removed her shoes. As she

climbed up, he mentioned to her that if she fell not to scream, and do it butt-first so he could catch her.

As she scooted up the tree, she paused and shook her head down at her father. Her weight to power ratio and athletic body allowed her to show up her dad quite nicely. She went to work sawing off a nut one at a time. As they fell, he caught each one. After cutting a few, she dropped the knife down to the ground and gradually slid down the tree.

"That was amazing! You are like a gecko." John poked at her and grinned.

"It was nothing and you should not compare women to lizards."

"My mistake. How about a cute monkey?"

"Keep your day job, Dad," Alexa laughed back at him.

"Which is currently being the master of cracking coconuts, so let's give it a try." John spoke over his shoulder as they scampered back to their camp and prepared for their feast.

He approached the log Alexa had slept by and took a few stabs into the wood, creating a hole. Flipping the knife over, he placed it in the hole with the blade facing up. He smacked the coconut on the blade, cutting through the fibrous outer husk. With each stab, the husk separated enough for him to strip pieces off. Once down to the fruit, he removed the knife and drilled a hole in the dark brown nut by twisting the knife.

"It is all for you. I had plenty to drink while you were napping," he offered politely.

The sweet milk was unlike anything Alexa had ever had before.

"Dad, you have to try this. It is one of the best things I have ever had!"

He leaned in, and took a small sip.

"Wow, that is super good! It certainly beats drinking

dusty dew from a leaf."

When the milk was gone, he cracked the nut and handed it to her with the knife. "I can't keep my eyes open any longer, sweetheart," he mumbled. John laid down and he pulled up the leaves around his body. Moments later, his breath evened and the slightest hint of a snore brought a smile to Alexa's face.

Alexa sat with her back to a tree and watched downhill to the path and listened to the birds while she snacked on the fruit. It was the first time since the death of her mother that she felt content. She was loved and almost wished that this was a deserted island. A new place and a new life that she could start. She dreamed of a beautiful hut she and Dad could build. As he hunted, she would gather fruits and vegetables from their garden. She would also frequently swim with dolphins, playing most of the day. Her day dreams shortly became real dreams as Alexa also nodded off, too tired to stay awake.

The wind picked up and rustled the canopy above the two sleeping travelers and woke Alexa... She opened her eyes, still resting with her back against the tree. She rubbed her face and her eyes to remove the dust from her tear ducts. The rhythmic motion of the tops of the trees in the wind was mesmerizing. At this vantage point, she could see the precise wind patterns within the swirls of the leaves. The wind was much fiercer than it had been, but the breeze was cool.

"How long have I been asleep?" John questioned as he opened his eyes and took in the view of the canopy.

"I am not sure, I dozed off, but the sun is right there and it is definitely cooler now." Alexa pointed off in the distance, trying to change the subject. She knew nodding off put them in danger.

Looking at his face, she saw disapproval at first, and then it turned to understanding. He nodded to her and then smirked. She failed his expectations, but this time it turned out okay. She winked back apologetically, and they discussed the plan of attack, keeping in mind that they were still being hunted.

It would only be a matter of time before they ran into their pursuers. A defensive position would be the best approach. They discussed how they would sleep in shifts now that they had at least some decent rest. John explained the priority was getting to a lookout point and finding a constant source of water.

The wind picked up once more and they looked up, creating a silence in the conversation. John pushed himself up from a seated position, stood, and stretched his tight muscles. She followed suit. Alexa joined his side as they made the trek up the path.

The sun was at their right, descending alongside the island, giving away the western direction. "It must be around four o'clock in the afternoon and the people chasing us would be close," he said quietly to her.

The trail tapered down to a few feet wide, and they proceeded with John in front and Alexa at the rear. The trees and vines above thinned out, giving way to the undergrowth which flourished and narrowed the path. He explained to her that the opening above must have been recent, as he pointed to a huge tree fallen off the path.

Suddenly there was a loud cry and a scurry in the trees. A monkey had spotted them. Without hesitation, the monkey sounded the alarm to his troop of primates up the hill. John stopped and ducked down, putting his arm over Alexa's shoulders.

§§§

"Let's go. We have to pass through their area before those men hear the calls!" John spoke quietly and they both sprinted up the path. The trees and vines whizzed by as they darted uphill with Alexa following her father's every step and leap but she was falling behind. Her lungs burned by the time the monkey calls subsided.

"Dad, I can't keep this pace. I am dying back here," she panted and placed her hands on her knees.

"Okay, I'll go little slower," John said and he reached down for her hand. Determined, she nodded and they were on their way.

A few moments later, the jungle opened up to a

plateau three quarters of the way up the mountain in the shape of a large semi-circle, and the path cut right through the middle. John paused at the edge, and Alexa came up alongside him. She bent over and put her hands on her knees as she took air into her lungs with huge gulps.

"This will be a good spot," he said, "because the monkeys will warn us of anyone approaching from that direction. This opening will allow us to see who is coming, as well. I expect those men from last night will come back for us."

"So where would we wait for them?"

"Straight ahead is the best viewing point. That is where anyone will expect us to be. So we can put traps along the straightaway and hide over there," John said, pointing right.

Alexa agreed that was definitely a less conspicuous place to hide, and she gave her father the thumbs up. He stated that they could make a shelter just beyond a healthy bush that would allow them to peer through and see the whole open area.

"We left a lot of footprints," he said, catching his breath. "So let's continue them straight across and turn left at the end of the area. At that point, we can double back, cover our tracks, and head to our real location, our actual vantage point."

§§§

They took extra-hard steps, breaking and snapping the plants along the side so the followers would notice the tracks. When they reached the end, he cut off a chunk of bamboo and fashioned a few spikes. He doubled back in the straight line to the entrance of the plateau and dug out a one-foot-deep hole and tossed the dirt far off to the side.

"I'm going to point several sharpened bamboo sticks towards the center of the hole. It will pierce the foot and ankle, slowing the victim down," John said while he made several openings in the sides of the hole, angling toward the center. Placing the sharpened bamboo stakes in the openings, pointy-side toward the middle of the hole, he followed up by covering the trap with a small weave of bamboo strips, earth, and leaves.

Cleaning up his extra footprints, he made his way back to Alexa, who was stripping some bamboo and vines to make a tripwire.

"That looks perfect," he told her. "Now braid them tightly so it is strong and eight feet long."

As Alexa tore off more strips and wove them together in a long line, he whittled up some larger spikes.

"We will create a whip that will have spikes like a triceratops," John said as he cut a supple piece of bamboo fifteen feet in length. He used the knife to cut some holes in the bamboo to insert the spikes.

He placed the whip at the end of the straightaway and tied it back with a quick slip knot. Alexa passed him the long woven line and he secured it to the knot. With the remaining line grasped in his hand, he stepped to the side of the path and gave it a tug releasing the knot holding the bamboo. The whip came thrashing into the path at such awesome speed that both of them stepped back in shock. However, it was a little too high. John sighed and adjusted its height. They pulled and secured the whip once more and set the trip line. Finally, he set the spikes in the whip and it was ready.

With the two traps in place, they covered their tracks and threw out the scraps from the bamboo into the thick of the jungle floor. Starting at the straightaway, they walked to the right, careful not to disturb any plants or leave any tracks. Once at their chosen vantage point, they looked over the open area and took a seat behind a large bush.

"There are a few things that could happen. One, both, or neither of the men fall for the trap," John said. "But what do we do in each case?"

Waiting for her answer, John inspected his daughter's expression. "I can see that you are in deep thought. What is occupying your mind?"

"I just can't determine if this is the right thing to do. I mean attempting to talk to them could lead to our death.

You heard them."

"Absolutely," John said.

"But injuring them will most likely slow, but not stop, them, and the worse thing is that they will be angry. Angry and more driven to kill us. Is the only answer to kill them, Dad?"

He grinned at her and she looked back at him with a scowl, showing her annoyance at his reply.

John held up his hand to stop her thoughts. "Oh, don't get me wrong, sweetie. It was not the subject matter; it was the way you thought of it. You are so much like your mother. You are a brilliant strategist and yet, the most humane."

"Thanks, but I suppose that gets us no closer to the right answer. Killing is wrong."

"In this case, I am not sure, but I believe you are at least missing one option. Separate them. Capture and question one of them to discover their actual intent and motivation."

"Well, that is probably not all that possible without digging a huge hole. Come on, Dad!"

They both smiled at each other. It was not really all that possible to separate them, or likely to happen with their limited time and resources.

"This brings up a good avenue to solve tough challenges. Have you heard of William Ockham?" John questioned, and she shook her head. "He was a theorist who had an idea to make decisions based on the fewest assumptions. I appreciated his defensive point of view. When you have more than one possible solution, choose the one with the fewest assumptions, if they are equivalent in effort. First, do we consider our options equal, in a sense?" he wondered.

"Sure, they are all pretty close, but I'll play along for the sake of discussion," she said, smirking and then poked him in the belly.

He let out a hissing sound and sucked in his stomach so it looked like it popped.

She let out a hearty laugh and fell backward, covering her mouth to stifle the noise.

After gaining their composure, they discussed each possibility, setting aside the count of assumptions that would make the plan a reality. Death was the most certain, with the least assumptions. In second place was injuring them with less-deadly traps, but it morally took the lead. Since it was possible to injure two of them, potentially separating the group, it held the best outcome. They decided to lower the whip trap to hit the victim in the legs.

The monkeys howled again. Alexa and John listened closely as the howls grew near. They were coming toward them. They had no time to finish preparing.

"They have seen our tracks," John said quietly, "and they will certainly quicken the pace. Quick, we need to make spears." As they scrambled to craft some spears, John spotted movement at the entrance of the path. He dove over to her and covered her mouth and turned her head toward the entrance.

Two men stepped out from the opening in the jungle.

CHAPTER 12

Bobby was shocked as he sat down in the sand. With one eye on Drondor, he thought deeply of the dead man's proclamation. How typical of Drondor to put the scare in everyone to gain power. Even in his death, he tormented the people around him. Shaking his head, his mind filled with fear, pondering the likelihood of Drondor's words.

"What did he mean when he said it was nice to meet me?" Bobby asked. "His lips didn't even move when he spoke. Was it even Drondor?"

"I don't know," Sergio said. "But I do know that no human could have thrown James like that. It knocked me down from six feet away. James is over two-hundred pounds. I'm no physics genius, but that's just not possible."

§§§

One year earlier. . .

Bobby's thoughts wandered to when he lost his best friend, Jules. Bobby believed deeply in the supernatural, as he often felt that Jules would visit him in his most needed moments.

He and Bobby got into trouble a lot together. On Bobby's seventeenth birthday, he was assigned to his cousin's squad of transporters. It was his first real job of moving drugs in the Philippines. Just as all the new transporters did, he had the childhood dissolution that being a smuggler was about fortune and fame. As a teen, his risk assessment was not fully developed, and he and Jules quickly overextended themselves.

The shipment was short and they knew it. Instead of being honest to the buyer, they lied, even though the amount of heroin was off by two and a half kilograms. They thought five and a half pounds wasn't that big of a deal when buying two-hundred and fifty. What they didn't realize it was worth nearly a half million credits at that time.

After they boarded the cruise liner, they relaxed from the anxiety of the transaction. They thought they were in the clear. They were wrong. The buyer discovered the discrepancy not long after they had left and sent a band of henchmen to capture and torture the four of them. Drondor and Joseph were the other two on this job and had been working with Bobby's father for years at this point.

The authorities stopped and boarded the cruise ship within an hour of departure. Neither Bobby nor Jules were afraid because they knew the police were paid off. Drondor would surely get them off the hook somehow. They imagined their time in custody would be short and painless, but their captors weren't the police.

As soon as the authority's boat was in progress, two gunshots rang out and echoed off the side of the cruise liner. Bobby flinched as the first bullet entered his gut and Jules bounced off the deck, taking the second to the neck. Bobby lunged out and cried, holding Jules's head in his arms.

The fake officers reached in and tried to pull Bobby off him, but he wouldn't let go of his best friend. The men managed to half-stand Bobby up, with Jules still in his arms, and pushed them backward off the boat. As Bobby surfaced with Jules, he heard one of the men curse as they sped off to the shore, leaving Bobby and Jules for dead. He screamed at the passengers of the cruise ship as the engines kicked in and pulled away. It didn't stop. No lifeboats were deployed.

Drifting a half mile off shore, Bobby held on tight with his arm around his friend's neck. The only thing in his mind was getting back to land. Both young men were losing tremendous amounts of blood.

Suddenly, he spotted shark fins nearby. Within minutes, dozens of man-killers came nearer and nearer in a frenzy. Bobby paddled frantically with one arm.

The first bump came in hard. The impact pushed them nearly fifteen yards. Screaming and thrashing, he tried to paddle. The sharks struck fast, tearing Jules from his arms. Blood bubbled in the ocean as his best friend's body was devoured. Parts flew as he was torn to pieces.

Bobby fell into unconsciousness.

Bobby opened his eyes. He was sitting at a table with Jules. All sounds were muffled and Jules was shaking Bobby's arm.

"Bobby, over here! Are you with me?"

The sound cleared up gradually, and Bobby looked beyond his friend Jules to the room. There seemed to be no floors or walls—just light gray that went on forever. Bobby's stomach turned as he looked down, afraid of falling off his chair. Jules snapped his finger and Bobby turned back to his direction.

"Over here, Bobby! I need you to do something for me."

"Am I dead? Are we dead?"

"It doesn't matter. Try to pay attention," Jules directed him.

"No really, what the hell is going on? You were torn apart by sharks and I have a huge hole in my stomach."

"No, you don't. Well at least not here, buddy."

"What's going on?" Bobby looked down and saw there was no gunshot wound.

"I'm dead, but you aren't. That doesn't matter right now. I need you to go back."

"Why?" Bobby pleaded.

"You will serve him. Go back!" Jules screamed as he stood up from the table. He leaned over, pushing Bobby backward off the chair. Bobby's eyes widened and his stomach fluttered as he fell from the dream.

Bobby woke a hundred meters from the shore, blood all around him. He choked up sea water. Floating on his back for a moment, he regained his composure and stopped gaging. Waves pounded him as he got closer to the shoreline and tumbled him in the undertow. Finally, he made it past the deep water and crawled his way up to the beach.

§§§

Bobby returned from his reverie and stood back up in the sand, looking down over Drondor.

"Let's find the other survivors. Maybe they have food and supplies, but first things first, we need to take care of this," Bobby called out, nodding toward the bodies of Drondor, James, and George. He instructed Sergio to gather any dry timber to build a funeral pyre.

Trip by trip, they laid out a large rectangle of logs, sticks, and dry undergrowth from the floor of the jungle. After three hours of tiring work, they hefted the three men's bodies onto the pyre, laced with oil from the outboard motor of the survival boat. Bobby lit the pyre.

He and Sergio sat back in the sand and watched as the remains of Drondor, James, and George sank away into the earth. After a period, the wind picked up, and the stench of human flesh was unbearable. They decided there was no better time to leave and find two thieves who stole their drugs.

They walked into the shadows close to the jungle, where the sand was firm and easier to traverse. After an hour of tramping through the sand, they found a freshwater spring on the beach bubbling up and snaking down to the sea. The hole was only a foot wide, but the water was crystal blue and cool as the ocean breeze. Kneeling, they cupped their hands and took turns drinking until they quenched their thirst. Fully refreshed, they decided to rest and strip down to their undergarments and wash their bloodied clothes in the ocean.

They rinsed their garments in the freshwater hole and hung them to dry on a branch at the jungle's edge. They rested in the sun, as the rays turned the corner of the island

and shown the length of the beach. Both men fell fast asleep, as it had been over a day since they had last rested.

§§§

Bobby was startled awake by the rush of water underneath him. The tide was coming in.

"Wake up, man," he said, as he shook Sergio's shoulder. "We've got to get going. It's going to be dusk in a few hours."

"Come on, Bobby. I just fell asleep, and what's the rush anyway?"

"You actually slept most of the day, but we'll get torched out here in the sun, or pulled back into the sea by the tide, so we might as well sleep on the jungle's edge."

"Fine, let's go," Sergio snapped. They gathered their clothes which were already bone dry. As Bobby put on his pants, a snapping sound, and a slight rustling up ahead in the direction they were traveling, caught him off guard. A vine securing the opening to a path broke loose. Bobby raised his brows as he walked over to the opening in disbelief.

"The jungle just opened up a door," Sergio said, then

he laughed. "Hmm, I don't hear any creepy music, so I think it's safe."

"Famous last words," Bobby said, ruefully.

"There are no tracks leading up the path, but the plants here in the entrance to the path were recently planted. You can tell because the soil is pressed up around the stalks of the plants." Bobby's suspicions rose to a climax.

"Someone did this to cover the entrance?" Sergio questioned, as he leaned down and inspected a large fern.

"They covered their tracks. Look at the uniform lines in the sand, as if it was swept."

"Seriously?" Sergio asked.

"You can see it right there." Bobby pointed to the trail a few feet away.

"No, Bobby. I can see now you're all ramped up and ready to go. I've had almost no sleep, and now you're going all crazy about tracking them down. Can't we just get some sleep?" he pleaded.

"You're a pansy, Sergio. Let's go while the trail is hot."

"No. I'm lying right here and going nowhere until I

get some more rest."

"And what happens when they come back down the path and see us sleeping here? It's obvious they don't want us to find them, so what happens when they find us? Think they'll want to cuddle?"

"Fine. What do you suggest, boss man?" Sergio laid on the sarcasm thickly.

"They have our drugs, Sergio. We'll find them and see if they have any communication off this island," Bobby snarled.

"Whatever. Let's go."

"And then we'll kill them for stealing our drugs," Bobby growled.

Both men headed up the path. Sergio leaned down and snagged a walking stick. He pulled out his newly acquired blade—the same blade Drondor used to kill his friend the evening before. He shaved the leaves and small branches off the stick and whittled a handhold as they walked up the path.

The sun rose high in the sky, and as the morning's dew evaporated, the humidity increased to uncomfortable levels. Sergio didn't forget to complain often and loud.

With a scowl on his face, Bobby turned and whacked Sergio with a branch across the knuckles. He'd had enough of Sergio's complaining.

"Ouch! What the hell, Bobby?" Sergio rubbed his wounded hand and kicked some sand at Bobby.

"Shut up! Just shut the hell up! I am in the same situation as you but you don't hear me whining about it like a sissy," Bobby yelled.

"That hurt! I'm going to whack you in the balls when you're sleeping," Sergio told him as he scowled.

"Well, that would feel better than your constant nagging and crying," Bobby talked back to him. "I nearly slipped back there on a puddle of your tears."

Sergio made a fist then released it. "Excuse me to—"

A shriek from the trees rang out. It was a troop of monkeys, whose warning calls were repeated far up the path.

"Look! Human tracks!" Bobby exclaimed. "They totally took off running and didn't bother covering them."

"You're right, and now I suppose you want me to run," Sergio said, mocking him.

"Hurry up. They have our drugs and we need to figure out how to get off this island," Bobby commanded.

Sergio rolled his eyes, threatened Bobby as he lifted his walking stick, ready to smack his friend.

"Stop! We need to go. They know we're onto them now. We need to close the gap," Bobby urged.

Sergio agreed by taking a deep breath and nodding to Bobby. "Fine, then."

"Give me the knife and you have your stick." Bobby jerked the blade from his hand.

"I hope you fall on it," Sergio snapped under his breath, as Bobby turned and sprinted up the hill.

"Oh, crap. Slow down!" Sergio yelled out as he tried to keep pace. He was not as fit as Bobby. After a few moments, Bobby looked over his shoulder and let up on his speed a bit so Sergio could catch up. Just as his comrade reached him, the path disappeared as it opened to a plateau.

They stopped a moment, as Sergio reached out and grabbed Bobby's arm.

"Hold up… Hold up." He panted, as he tried to get the words out. Bobby scanned the area. It was quiet. Too quiet. He looked down at the footprints leading through the tall weeds straight ahead.

"This way," Bobby instructed, as the two moved forward cautiously.

CHAPTER 13

Hours earlier. . .

Rusty cursed as he tossed a thick rope over the bow of the ship. Hand over hand, he climbed down. Within a few feet of the ground, he let go and landed backward in the sand. Defeated, Rusty sat up, with his knees to his chest and held in head in his hands. Replaying his encounter with the drowning woman, Rusty felt responsible for her fate.

Did I kill the woman from my dream? Over and over, Rusty questioned his actions. Maybe if he tried to resuscitate her longer, she would have lived. If he hadn't panicked when she clawed at him, he could have pulled her to the surface sooner. He could have saved her.

Lucky nudged him, and he wiped his tears and talked with the pig about the woman. The pig replied to his sad conversation with a prance, tossing sand high in the air as if trying to coax him out of his self-loathing. *Lucky is right.* It was over. Nothing at this point would bring the woman back.

He wiped the sand from his clothes as he walked to the waterfall one slow step after another. The night had passed and he hadn't closed his eyes once. He gradually took off his garments and washed them in the pristine pond and hung them on the edge of the jungle over a large vertical vine he secured to a sapling. He lay on a rock by the pond and stared off at the canopy while his clothes dried. The warm breeze comforted him, and he gradually nodded off only to be awoken some time later by Lucky. With a quick snort, his attention turned to the pig. As he turned to lie back down, the pig snorted again, this time louder.

"What is it?" he called to her with a yawn.

With her nose to the ground, Lucky kicked up sand and shook her head.

"Did you find something?" he inquired, as he sat up and noticed the outline of a track under her nose. He hopped to his feet and scampered over for a closer look. This was not an animal track. It was a human footprint.

Cemented in the silt by the pond, the print was well preserved. He carefully brushed the leaves and sticks from it and traced the outline of the impression. It was weathered and faded and appeared to be there for a while. For comparison, he placed his foot near the indent. The hairs rose on the back of his neck as he realized it was the same size. Pressing down into the fossil, his heart raced. It was an exact match. Question after question flooded his mind. How long has he been here? Why was there not a permanent shelter nearby if he'd been here before? Where were all his possessions and why was the beach not looted? He placed his hand on his head, swaying as he sat back down on the rock, trying to comprehend this discovery.

"How long have I known you, Lucky?"

Lucky responded with wide, comforting eyes and rubbed her snout in his hand.

"Ahh, I understand. I didn't build a shelter here because I built it somewhere else. That means there must be a better spot somewhere on this island. Where would I choose to build it?"

Lucky sprinted back out to the beach and snorted and Rusty followed along. He was becoming familiar with her ability to communicate. As he reached the spot where she stopped, halfway between the cruise ship and the waterfall, he pondered what she was trying to tell him.

Lucky turned back to where they had come from, snorted, and wiggled.

"I don't see what you are trying to say," Rusty remarked with a frown. He raised his head as he took in the view of the top of the jungle and all the way up to the two mountain peaks in the distance. He noticed something out of the ordinary, drifting beyond the edge of the jungle. Just to the right of where the waterfall rested, high above the tree line, smoke tapered off into the sky. Whatever made the smoke was on the other side of the island from where he stood.

"That smoke is on the southern tip of the island, where the obelisk is!" Rusty exclaimed.

He took off running and gathered supplies to make the trip across to the other side. Lucky scampered back and forth, evidently happy that Rusty finally understood what she was trying to say.

Minutes later, Rusty had put together some gear and started jogging south, down the edge of the water, toward the smoke. By the time he would be close to the origination of the fire, it could be out. He had to make haste. He had to know who started this fire. *Could the woman from my dream still be alive?*

CHAPTER 14

Rusty broke his way across the southern side of the island and discovered the dreadful source of the fire. Covering his face at the pungent stench of human flesh, he stepped carefully toward the pyre and kept his eyes on the jungle edge, watching for movement.

Two unanchored boats drifted a hundred yards off shore. A lot of footprints led from the shore to the smoldering fire. The pyre sat in the center of the beach, measuring a dozen feet wide and equally as long. Thick, dark smoke rose far into the sky and was disbursed by the wind hundreds of feet above Rusty.

His stomach turned at the sight of the torched bodies smoldering in the pile of coals. Convulsing, he grasped at this mouth to hold back from vomiting as he witnessed the blackened skin and flesh dripping into the coals. Turning away to gather his composure, he knelt and took a few deep breaths to calm the hammering of his heart against his ribs.

There was no telling how these people died, for their bodies were destroyed. Nothing could determine if they died of an injury or were murdered. As Lucky joined his side, he looked toward the bay to the boats. They were the same as the ones located on the side of the larger ship he had explored earlier. They were probably passengers before the shipwrecked.

"I imagine burning bodies would be a matter of respect, wouldn't you say, Lucky?"

Lucky put in her opinion by running up the beach in the direction of tracks leading away. She snorted, and hopped around, urging him to get moving. Rusty decided it would be best to secure one of the boats to look for more clues to the incident and just in case he needed one on this side of the island.

He jumped into the warm water with a quick splash and ducked his head under an oncoming wave. Surfacing, he sprayed out saltwater from his mouth as he pushed himself at full steam and chased down the boat. Rusty approached and edged his way along the side of the craft toward the stern. Grasping on to the cold railing, his muscles tightened as he pulled himself up to his belly on the back of the boat. He lifted each of his legs haphazardly as the waves tossed him off balance and he rolled into the deck. There were no humans aboard, but there was blood. Dark brown splotches and pools stained the seat and specks led over the port side. Something violent happened here. *Murder.*

Reaching down, he picked up a single oar and awkwardly attempted to paddle toward shore. Waves rocked the boat and smacked the oar against the side, throwing off his balance. After a few hundred strokes, swapping back and forth from port to starboard side, he angled the boat toward shore, and it beached with a loud scrape. He grabbed a long rope, tied it off to a large log resting near the pyre, and turned his attention to Lucky.

"That should keep it still, little partner," Rusty suggested as he reached down and rubbed the pig's sides.

Retrieving his supplies, with his machete in hand, he

jogged north, past the obelisk, as he followed the tracks up the beach.

As the sun rose high overhead, Rusty stopped short. He saw two sleeping men. He literally caught them with their pants down. Rusty and Lucky stopped at the edge of the jungle, peered out from behind some large leaves, and sized up the two snoozers.

"Shh, little girl. Be very quiet. We need to find out what these guys are up to before we attempt to make friends." Rusty looked into Lucky's eyes and saw that she was not happy.

"They're not good people, are they?" Rusty scratched Lucky's chin.

Lucky jutted her chin as she stared back into Rusty's eyes.

Rusty and Lucky remained quiet and waited at the edge of the jungle until the tide finally found the men. He inched his way closer, trying to hear their conversation, but their words were muffled at his distance.

"Stay here, Lucky. I'll be right back," He whispered to the pig and snuck closer, staying low to the ground and shielded by the undergrowth. The men stood suddenly and walked right for Rusty's location. He froze as the two walked directly toward him. His heart beat in his ears, and sweat poured from his shaking limbs. Silently, he pulled the stalk of a large leaf to conceal him from view and lay down flat.

Just as the men arrived at the edge of the jungle, they stopped. One man reached out and pulled down their clothes from the tree. Rusty let out his breath slowly as he realized he'd been holding it for too long. The men put on their shirts, and as the last one pulled up his pants, a rustling sound up ahead in the jungle caught everyone's attention. The two men jerked their heads in the direction of the noise.

Rusty quietly followed along parallel to them in the jungle until he saw the opening and stopped. He dropped to a prone position and held perfectly silent. He could now hear their words. One of them was complaining about being tired. The other man called the complainer Sergio. He then called his companion Bobby. Rusty was also clued in to the fact that they were following someone. They weren't happy.

The men ventured into the opening and stopped mere feet from Rusty's hiding spot. He had come too close. He should have known they would turn the corner and go up the path. The last words gave away their real position in this chase.

"And then we will kill them for stealing our drugs," the man called Bobby said loud and clear.

The men traveled up the path. A moment later, Rusty stood as they walked out of sight. He called to Lucky. The pig responded in her sneakiest trot through the undergrowth. Not even the slightest sound was heard. As the pig came closer to his side, Rusty leaned down and scratched behind her ears.

"You are a good little girl, you know?" Rusty complimented her as he admired the swine's sneakiness. "Let's follow these two up the mountain and see who they are hunting." They set out after the men.

§§§

Rusty and Lucky crested the hill and the path opened to a plateau. Lucky, with Sergio in sight, squealed and took off like a rocket. With blazing speed, the boar charged, snarling and grunting. Rusty froze as Lucky blasted toward the two.

Sergio backpedaled and his foot sank down into a hole. Screaming in agony, sharpened bamboo spikes punctured his foot and ankle. His body fell backward and leaves sprung in the air. His arms flailed and he slammed into the ground. Sitting up fast, Sergio scurried backward in an attempt to get away from the charging boar. Lucky clamped down on his injured foot, cutting straight through the leather of his shoe and into his flesh. Shaking his head back and forth, Sergio winced, bore his teeth, and kicked the boar with his free foot.

Bobby stepped to the side and readied his knife to slam it into the pig's back. At the same time, Sergio grasped and tugged at his walking stick. It was caught on something. With a tug, he sprung a second trap. The trigger was connected to a taut piece of bamboo held under tension.

Thrashing in, a bamboo branch smacked Bobby in the back of his legs and knocked him off his feet.

Sergio jerked forward as he received the full force of the blow. His body shook as sharpened spikes at the end of the branch buried in his back and came out of his chest.

Scampering to his feet, Bobby made his way to Sergio's side. Bloodied tips of sharpened bamboo protruded from Sergio's chest, funneling out sickening amounts of blood into his lap.

What started out as a low grumble from Sergio quickly increased into a horrific battle cry as he stumbled to his feet. His stick whistled in the wind as he brought it down and cracked the pig in the head. His face red, he looked up at Rusty. Step after awkward step, Sergio drug his mutilated foot behind him. He raised his stick high above his head as he moved closer, increasing rage and speed. As he stepped forward, the slack from the branch became taught like a leash and jerked him off balance. The force pulled him sideways, and he landed face-first in the dirt at Rusty's feet.

Rusty looked down at Sergio's now lifeless body and then back up to the man called Bobby. With a slight pause, Bobby burst from the ground and charged Rusty with the silver blade held high in the air.

"No!" A young woman screamed as a middle-aged man darted out from the bush and sprinted toward the fight, armed with a knife.

Bobby thrashed, but Rusty parried the attack away and returned with a swipe of the machete. He swung the blade in a wide arc at Bobby's midsection. With a side step, Bobby dodged the swipe only to be tackled to the ground by the man from the trees.

Both men hit the ground and the knife sprang free within the cloud of dirt and leaves as it launched into the air. Bobby came up with his own knife, but the man snatched his wrist and landed a quick, blinding jab to Bobby's nose. The man secured Bobby's position with a knee into his throat and grasped Bobby's knife hand.

Bobby suddenly let go of the knife, and as the man's eyes followed the blade to the ground, Bobby pulled him forward and kicked hard into his groin. Stunned from the shot, the man fell to his side, and Bobby snatched the knife off the ground. With one quick thrust, Bobby buried it into the man's thigh as a spirt of blood sprayed Bobby's face. The man screamed out in pain as Bobby twisted the knife.

With the machete blade turned sideways, Rusty smacked the side of Bobby's face, throwing him to the ground with a loud crack. Terror filled Bobby's eyes as he turned to see Rusty raise the blade. With a swift kick to the inside of Rusty's knee, Bobby dropped him to the ground, stood, and bolted down the path.

As Bobby fled, the woman darted out of the bush and skidded to her knees over to the man.

"We need to wrap that fast," she exclaimed.

"Take this," Rusty offered as he sliced a strip from his shirt and passed it to the woman.

"Thank you. I'm Alexa and this is my father, John. We appreciate your help." Alexa snatched the cloth and went to work on her father's leg.

"Yes, we really appreciate your help," John added, wincing. "It could have been a lot worse if you and your friend over there didn't show up."

"I'm Rusty Mechanic and I believe you were the hero here. That fine lady is Lucky."

"Who, me?" Alexa asked, not seeing the reference to the pig.

"Ha! I was referring to the girl with the tusks resting over there," Rusty corrected her as he walked over to check on his swine friend.

Lucky stood with a snort and wiggled as Rusty stroked her back and looked at the bump on her head.

"She took a nasty shot to the head. Is she okay?" John spoke with a yelp at the pain, as Alexa tightened the tourniquet.

"She'll do fine, I'm sure. How does that leg feel?" Rusty asked after a quick inspection.

"It's seen better days. We'll know when the bleeding stops, I guess," John's voice quivered as Alexa gave it the last knot.

"What kind of name is Rusty Mechanic?" Alexa asked.

"Well, that is a long story. Actually, it's pretty short. I don't remember much at all. I woke up on the beach a few days ago, and I don't remember who I am. I found this shirt and I'm using this name for now."

"You're serious, aren't you?" John asked him and raised an eyebrow at the odd story.

Rusty replied with a nod and continued telling them the start of his new existence. He covered the beach, the jellyfish sting, the first shack that burned, traveling up the path, the grove of pineapples, the darkened beings, and the ship.

"That sounds like the cruise ship we were on," John interjected and Alexa confirmed by asking Rusty what it looked like.

Rusty continued with the smoke, and how he and Lucky traveled the southernmost tip of the island, the funeral pyre with three bodies, stumbling on the two men and following them to this point.

"Five men. Three in the fire, and one dead right there. That guy's alone now," John counted out loud.

"Oh, so you met these guys before?" Rusty wondered. John told him of the night the cruise ship was swallowed by a typhoon.

Alexa confirmed his count and Rusty drew a map in the sand of what he knew. John commented on the sand sketch of Rusty's rendering of the island. It was in the shape of a heart. All three agreed it would be best to travel to the wrecked cruise liner in search of supplies for John's leg. Rusty suggested they move up the path to get to the ship quicker, rather than travel down the path the way he had come.

Alexa and John agreed it was a better way, and Alexa and Rusty pulled John to his feet to test his mobility.

"I'll be honest. It's not good. I think the bleeding is mostly controlled, but I won't be able to put much pressure on it," John stated and explained his idea to fashion some crutches.

They all went right to work. Rusty chopped two foot-long pieces of thick bamboo shoots, and Alexa carved a hole in each chute with John's knife. They scavenged two long, straight sticks and made a 'T' with each, by placing the hole in the bamboo shoots onto the top of the long sticks.

John tried them out. The bamboo crutches worked well. John commented on their craftsmanship and thanked both.

"You're welcome," Rusty and Alexa replied in unison. Both blushed as they looked at each other and then back to John.

"Okay, let's get going." John headed off on his bamboo crutches and they walked to the far edge of the opening. They discovered a path leading away in the direction of the ship, but the undergrowth had nearly consumed it. The path remained level and there wasn't a good view downward at this point.

"I assume this covered path leads back to the beach," Rusty stated. "We should see the ship in no time."

They all agreed, and Rusty set off first to carve a path for the other two with his machete.

After a period, they stopped under the full cover of the jungle and rested. John inspected his armpits which were already showing abrasions from the crutches.

Rusty took off his shirt and wrapped it around the left crutch to provide some padding. Alexa's mouth gaped slightly and John quickly gave her a stern look, and Rusty tried not to notice. She took the remains of John's shirt and wrapped the second crutch, and they were back on their way.

Alexa led this section of the jungle where the path was now intact and free from the intruding plants. The path led them to a small opening which gave them a great view out and down to the eastern side of the island.

"I can see the entrance to the path leading down to the waterfall out over there." Rusty pointed. A deep valley lay between them and the path entrance, ensuring that they couldn't take a direct route.

"I'm not sure this path links up, but it's going to get us close. What do you two think?" John asked.

"Honestly, we'll get there eventually, but it's all up to how your leg is, Dad."

"Yes, what does your leg say?" Rusty added.

"Well, it looks like the bleeding stopped, so let's continue," John replied, looking down at the wound.

"Dad, I don't need you to be a hero. Is it really okay for you to continue?"

"Yes, it's fine, but we're not going to make it all the way to the beach today, so let's go until we find a place to rest."

They continued down the path until the density of the canopy blocked out the remaining rays of the sun and made it difficult to see. Slowly creeping along, they trudged through the jungle until it opened onto a second plateau. As they entered the opening, they stopped in shock. There stood a well-built bamboo cabin.

"Wait here, Alexa," John warned, as she picked up her pace toward the discovery. "We don't know if there's anybody there."

"I think it's deserted, Dad."

"Still . . . Rusty, will you go and check it out?"

Rusty turned to them and bowed, placing his left hand across his waist while raising his right hand in the air. Both John and Alexa let out a laugh at his show. He turned and crouched low with his machete still in hand and crept up to the cabin. Halfway to the building, he turned and stood up sharp.

"Why am I crouching?" he whispered rhetorically, and Alexa let out a rather loud laugh.

John tried to stifle her outburst by waving his crutch at her, only making it worse.

Rusty tried his best to hold his mouth shut as he approached the cabin. His body convulsed as he attempted to subdue the laughter. He meant to stay serious, but each step he took made holding back the laughter even harder.

Finally, John burst out, unable to contain his

laughter at Rusty's poor attempt at a stealth maneuver.

Rusty nearly fell on his machete as he took a knee and then rolled over onto his stomach with laughter.

With the three in stitches, Lucky trotted right past Rusty up the stairs to the shack and walked right in the front door.

All three of them froze, waiting to see what would happen.

Lucky appeared a moment later in the doorway with a stuffed bear in her mouth.

Another large burst of laughter put all three of them rolling in the dirt at the sight of the pig who thought she was a dog. Rusty sat up a moment later with tears in his eyes, covered in mud, furthering Alexa's laughter.

John regained his composure and hobbled up to the house, leaving the two still in the dirt. "I suppose the element of surprise is just too serious for you two," John said, as he poked his head in. "This is what life is about," he yelled out and stepped inside.

Rusty and Alexa popped in the doorway to see John all sprawled out on a comfy bed in a spacious bedroom, which was crafted entirely of bamboo. The bed was made of stripped leaves, dried and soft.

"This place is great," Alexa said while glancing through the three rooms. One covered room in the center contained the bed. The room on the right had three walls and a roof, and it opened to the most glorious view of the ocean. High above everything else, they could see the path down to the beachhead.

"Dad, I can see our ship. I can see the path!" Alexa exclaimed.

"That's nice, dear, but I'm napping right now," John said jokingly.

"Actually, that's not a bad idea. You rest while Rusty and I check this place out," Alexa said, as Lucky jumped on the bed and laid down next to John.

"I think you made a friend there," Rusty added, as he sat down in the covered room, opened the lid to a trunk, and rummaged through it.

Alexa continued looking throughout the home. In the breezeway, she delved through each of the trunks. The first was packed with kitchen necessities: a single pot, a frying pan made from cast iron, and wooden utensils obviously not made from bamboo, six plates and matching blue ceramic bowls, and a box of fine silver utensils.

"Wow, this is nice and it is real silver," she stated as she looked over her shoulder to Rusty, peaking in the door. "These must have been salvaged from one of the ships on the shore."

"I seem to remember that. In fact, I'm pretty sure this is my place, Alexa."

"Really? You did all of this?"

"I think so. It seems all too familiar, and the clothes in the trunk in the other room are all my size. Oh, and there's a painting of me," Rusty gestured.

"What? Are you serious?" she questioned, wide-eyed, and then covered her mouth, trying not to wake her dad.

Rusty held up a painting of a man on a horse with a castle in the background. The resemblance was uncanny. "It is you, but that's s really old painting. It doesn't make sense."

"Well, maybe it's a distant relative," Rusty stated.

"Possibly, but that's considerably old and there's a castle in the background."

Rusty raised his eyebrow at her last statement. "What do you mean by that?"

"People haven't lived in castles for thousands of years, and there's no way that painting survived this long out here in the humid jungle. Ah, right there." Alexa pointed to the bronze nameplate at the bottom. "You can see this painting was painted for Sir Christopher Labelle in 1700."

"What year is it?" Rusty asked.

"326 AE. Why? What year did you think it was?"

"326! What does that mean? What does AE mean?" Rusty shouted with shock.

"It means 326 relative earth years. AE is After Earth."

Rusty shook his head and covered his face with his hands. "And what does *After Earth* mean exactly?"

"AE was added after AD, which was after the death of the Christian prophet Jesus."

"I am familiar with Jesus. When did AE start?"

"AE started when we left the planet in the year 2735 AD. 2736 then became 1 AE instead."

Something was wrong. Rusty shook his head. and muttered, "No, no," again and again as he buried his face in his hands.

Alexa reached out and gently took each of his hands in hers and carefully brought them down from his face. She looked him in his eyes, as he allowed tears to streak down his cheeks.

"It's going to be okay, Rusty," she said as she wrapped her arms around his shoulders. "It's going to be okay," she whispered in his ear.

He hugged her tightly, sobbing in confusion.

As she pulled away from him, she paused and placed a small kiss on his cheek and looked deeply into his eyes.

His sobbing stopped as he looked back at her. There was something about her. Her face reddened, and placed her fingers over her necklace.

CHAPTER 15

With a lucky jab, Bobby buried the knife in the attacker's leg and twisted the blade. As his victim yelped in pain, he withdrew the knife, kicked the other man in the leg and bolted down the path. With a quick look over his shoulder, he realized they weren't following him. His face felt flushed, and he clenched his hands around his knife as he cursed. He cursed for the sunken cruise ship, for his dead comrades, for being alone, for that damn boar, and for the two people who attacked him.

He could barely keep his eyes open as he thudded down the path. His lips were dry as a bone, and all he could think about was the brook at the water's edge. As he turned a corner, his foot caught a root and sent him flying. He let loose of the knife as he tumbled to the ground and rolled.

Dirt and leaves kicked up as he slid to a stop.

Bobby screamed as he punched the ground and made his way to his feet. He stood with his chest heaving and heart raging in frustration.

"I'm going to kill them!" Over and over he mumbled this mantra. He bore his teeth and clenched his fist as he searched for the knife. A quick glimmer of steel caught his eye and he snatched the blade and sped back down the path as he continued his chant. "I'm going to kill them."

Hours later, the sun had set and the moon was high above the island reflecting a silver sheen across the water. Bobby broke out of the path like a bullet from a gun and darted toward the spring just in time as the tide nearly covered it. Quickly, he splashed water everywhere and submerged his head beneath the water. Gulp after gulp he sucked in the spring as fast as he could, all the while continuing the chant in his mind.

With the moon at his side, he walked north away from his attackers, away from the life raft and the burning corpses. Hours passed, and his eyes hung heavy as his feet scraped over the top of the shore. His limbs tensed and shook at the strain of hiking up the mountain and running back down only to continue through the deep sand.

Falling to his knees, he cried out, shook his head and raised his fists at the sky. His scream echoed off the edge of the jungle, sending a cloud of bats high in the air.

"I will kill them!" Bobby let out a thunderous roar at the sight of the colony of bats.

As he brought his hands down, he rested them on his leg and noticed a bump. He fumbled in his pockets and produced a lighter and some keys. He launched the keys into the oncoming tide and spiraled to the ground. Rolling over on his back, he reached his hands high and shook the lighter. *Half full.*

With his last energy, he gathered some small sticks and leaves and built a quick fire by the edge of the trees. As he continued his deadly chant, he sharpened the tip of his spear, baring his teeth with every stroke. Hardening the edge in the fire, he sat back and brushed off the soot from the new weapon. Echoes of wild laughter reflected off the land as he fantasized of murder.

Noises from the jungle floor aroused his suspicion.

"I see you! Come on, come and get me!" he yelled out into the darkness, but no one was there. Blinded by the campfire light, shadows lurked in his mind as he scanned the area. There was something there. Armed with the knife in his left hand and spear in the right, he crouched low to the ground and scurried to the edge of the trees. Just north of him, shining in the moonlight were a set of eyes. His feet shuffled through the sand as he quietly stepped closer. *It is one of them! I will kill them.*

With a swoosh, he launched the spear and roared. sprinting at his target. The eyes blinked in the moonlight as the spear thudded into its body. Bobby slid to his knees over the top of the being and stabbed down with the knife. He plunged the blade and pummeled its face over and over. He had killed him. The man with the machete. The man with the boar.

But as the moonlight shined upon its face, he realized it was not the man. It was a monkey. Shaking and twitching, he collapsed in the sand and yelled, his frustration twisting his mind.

Up ahead, just north of his location, the moon shined

down on an inlet where the water traveled into the island. Fish jumped in the distance. Staggering, he got to his feet and wiped the saliva and blood from his mouth. His stomach grumbled as he picked up speed, charging toward the stream with blood and sweat in his tailwind.

He dove in with a big splash after a fish but missed. Surfacing, Bobby looked down the river which cut through the island from north to south, creating a huge cavern. The tide was high and he drifted into it, fully-clothed, until he was belly deep. A splash off to his left grabbed his attention. A rather large fish re-entered the water. He reached up with the knife in his hand and waded toward the location of the splash. He thrust the knife into the dark water.

"I'll get you, you bastard!" he yelled as he repeatedly thrashed at the waves. Over and over he stabbed down into the water. A moment later he froze as something slowly emerged from the water behind him, casting a huge shadow in front of him. He turned suddenly. His muscles tightened, and his heart thumped in fear as he watched a figure materialize before him.

The silhouette grew as it approached him slowly,

with his background perfectly lit in the moonlight. "What are you?" Bobby quivered, as he waded backward, trying to widen the distance from the thing that was coming up from the depths. Suddenly, the form's haziness cleared, leaving the shape of a man.

"I told you I would come for you, Bobby," the figure threatened.

With blazing speed, it lunged for Bobby and dragged him down under the waves.

Thrashing and choking, he tried to break free, but the figure held him down with incredible strength.

Over and over, the figure plunged Bobby's head into the ocean, filling his lungs with water. Bobby pleaded, clawed and hammered at the figure's chest, but his muscles weakened under the strain and soon he went limp. With his life at the edge, the monster lifted Bobby out of the incoming tide and threw him onto the shore.

"Please stop! Who are you?" Bobby pleaded, gasping and coughing out water and sand.

"With these souls of three, I will allow you to die in peace. Three and I will be alive!" the image screamed, disappeared briefly, then rematerialized before him, showing his face.

Bobby froze in terror as the figure's face came into view. It was Drondor.

"How can it be? You're dead! I burned your body!" Bobby cried frantically, as he backed away in the sand.

"You will call me master!" The voice boomed, and he raised his hands, generating wind and rain. Lightning struck all along the beach, and the wind whipped, picking up sand and pelting the pleading man.

"I will do as you ask, Master," Bobby complied, as he raised his eyes in the direction Drondor was pointing. Deep in the gorge was a fire in intense reds with dozens of legs circling the flames.

"They are yours to command, Bobby. Use them to bring the souls to me," the voice of Drondor instructed. "Build a fire and bring them to you."

"I don't understand!"

"Of course you don't, Bobby; I will give you the knowledge," the monster spoke in rhythms and grasped Bobby's head. Flashes of light broke from the heavens as the clouds separated and swirled. Bobby's head thrust back as the light reached his mind. Bobby shook wildly and screamed as the images of history were forced upon him. Thousands of years of memories flashed in his brain. It was not Drondor. It was someone else entirely.

Just as fast as the images came to him, everything disappeared. His body felt renewed and his mind was clear. He built a fire to summon his demons.

"I will kill them!" He screamed the loudest chant and continued it by softening into a smooth crescendo as he built his fire.

Bobby's dream melded into the present as he chanted and danced amongst the flames, calling to them. A low murmur began as the fire in the distance raged high in the sky. The legs stopped. They were looking in his direction. As each second passed, the sound gained in intensity, and Bobby could see through his sweat-covered brow.

They were coming. He raised his hands, palms upward to the sky as they neared. The group assembled around his fire, dancing and chanting, fueling the blaze.

They were black as night with a red hue. Chains and jewels adorning the creatures gleamed as they circled and praised Bobby.

Bobby instructed them to carry him back to their lair, to grow in strength and prepare for the harvest of souls. They lifted him high in the air with his chest to the sky and his arms outstretched. Trudging through the deep sand, they made their way back to the north. The pace was slow, and Bobby tried his power over them and urged them on, faster and faster. The wind picked up in coordination with the new pace, cooling his body and blowing through his hair as he was carried.

Deep in the gorge, they descended downward into their lair, two by two, with Bobby heading up the rear. The cave led down and to the left, circling lower and lower into the depths of the island. The smell of wood smoke was replaced in his senses with the stench of sweat and steel of the caverns. As he trudged downward, the light below him increased until the glow opened into a chasm—a deep and wide room. Lava pooled on the edges of this opening, and his minions worked weapons out of the flows, hammering war on anvils, deep and steady. Bobby was pleased with the immensity of the operation. He felt his success was imminent. *I will kill them!*

Suddenly smoke leaked out of the lava, and with a low gurgle it moved toward the center of the room and swirled. The beings bowed to the twisting smoke and chanted as the master took physical presence.

"I expect this is to your satisfaction, Bobby," the newly formed being said. "Here, you fashion destruction of enough power to do my simple deed. Wouldn't you agree?"

"I do, my lord." Bobby bowed at this demonic form. "Who are you?"

"Cretus is my name. Come hither and let me remind you of the rules," the master spat and held out a hand.

Bobby was lifted from the stairs and pulled by some unseen force toward the master. Suspended by his hair, Bobby screamed out as he tried to break free from the hold.

"You will kill them all or you will burn in eternity down here!" Cretus commanded and then suddenly disappeared into the smoke, dropping Bobby to the floor.

CHAPTER 16

Placing the painting back on the wall, Alexa and Rusty stepped outside to talk without waking John. Rusty started a small fire and they sat. Silver gleamed from her neckline as Alexa fingered the pendant, which shined in the firelight. Rusty tilted his head to the side and his cheeks flushed.

"It's beautiful, as are you," Rusty said.

Alexa's mouth curled into a shy smile at the compliment. She had never imagined such a moment. Rusty was handsome and kind and it was hard to believe she was sitting here right now. Tiny droplets of sweat broke on her back and arms, sending a shiver through her as the light breeze swept by.

"Tell me, where did you get that pendant? But first,

let me get you something. You look cold," Rusty said and stood, but she stopped him with her hand on his arm.

"It's okay. I got this robe from inside," she said, reaching down, producing a long black robe, which she quickly snuggled into. She pulled the hood up over her head and touched the necklace again. Alexa liked being near Rusty. A warmth and comfort came over her when he was near. She felt like she'd always known him. She took a deep breath to steady her voice and started the story of the necklace.

"It came from my mother. It was passed to me as it was once passed to her. The story goes that a long time ago, there was a scientist . . ." Alexa began.

§§§

Rusty listened to her talk about the scientist and the captain, as wisps of her blonde hair blew gently outside of her hood, sending him back to his dream. He could barely take his eyes off Alexa as the necklace glimmered and sparkled, dancing in the firelight. He knew. Rusty took a deep breath and reached for her hand. Alexa stopped her story and looked at him, surprised. She asked, "What is it?"

"It's you. The woman from my dreams," Rusty whispered and leaned closer.

Alexa gently removed her hood.

"What did you say?" she asked, as they stared into each other's eyes.

"I have dreamed of you for a thousand years," he whispered, with a quivering voice. Rusty raised his hand and brushed Alexa's cheek.

The necklace began to glow. As their lips met, their minds melted with a rush of energy coursing through them, transporting them to a faraway land. Their bodies and minds intertwined, circling in an abyss of stars and cosmic heavens.

With a gasp, their kiss broke and they opened their eyes to the small fire.

She looked into his eyes and he knew she had felt it, too. Without words, they walked to an open space by the fire and laid down. Both closed their eyes and Alexa finished the story of love. They were swept away in their dreams for the night.

§§§

Rusty woke to Alexa shaking him.

Hazy with sleep, he looked at her beautiful face. Seeing worry in her eyes, fear and suspicion set his mood. He looked away from her up to the sky as a wind whipped through the trees. The trees shook, throwing branches into the open area surrounding his cabin.

"They're coming," Rusty said quietly.

"What did you say, Rusty?"

"The last time the storm picked up, a huge boat landed on the shore."

"You should let me know more in advance when we're going to have visitors. I would have prepared something special," Alexa said in her best southern drawl.

Rusty stood and reached out a hand for Alexa and lifted her to her feet. Both walked without saying a word to check on John. As they climb the steps to the house, they saw the bed was empty.

"Dad! Dad!" Alexa called out frantically, as she entered the house.

"Well, it's about time, you two. I thought I was going to finish all this coffee by the time you both woke up," John said.

"Oh, what I wouldn't do for a cup of warm coffee right now," Alexa said

"No way. That'll stunt your growth, my dear." John teased.

"Dad, I'm seventeen, if you haven't forgotten. I've had coffee before," Alexa tossed back, crossing her arms.

"I'm only pulling your leg, but I wasn't kidding. Rusty does have coffee. We just need a way to brew it," John confirmed with excitement.

"Oh, that's easy. In the other room, I saw a pot to warm up some water, but we don't have any water," Alexa remarked.

John motioned his head to the side, and they both looked through the breezeway and sure enough, there was a stream.

"I guess there's a reason why I put this house here, besides the great view," Rusty said, chuckling.

Alexa scurried off into the other room to grab the pot. With a moment of clanging and banging, she reappeared in the doorway with a small cast iron kettle. She blew out the dust, smiled at Rusty and her father, and ran out the doorway down the steps to the stream. With a quick rinse, she filled the bucket and stirred up some warm coals from the night before.

"And just for good measure," Alexa announced, as she tossed a handful of sticks into the fire pit.

"Not too big now; a storm is coming," John yelled out. She hung the pot on a cross bar over the top of the fire. The bar was made of the same kind of dark black metal as the pot and it was perfectly positioned over the pit.

"Let's look at that leg now, Dad," Alexa suggested.

Still sitting in the chair in the breezeway, John leaned over and unwrapped the bandage made Rusty's shirt. Blood oozed from the open wound and down his leg.

"You're going to need some stitches, and I bet some antibiotics, as well," Alexa remarked, looking at the wound.

"Yes, definitely antibiotics. Um . . . What are antibiotics?" Rusty questioned.

John decided to field Rusty's new question with a lesson in basic biology. Then he suggested that the cruise ship would most likely have antibiotics still worth salvaging.

Whistling through the trees, the wind shook the leaves. Shining in the daylight, the canopy looked like a green sequined blanket. Watching the storm gradually increase, they all agreed it was risky to venture to the ship, but they had no idea how long the storm would last, and John badly needed to close the wound.

Rusty volunteered, stating that he didn't mind a little weather if they could explain exactly what it is that he would be looking for.

With careful imagery, John described the layout of the ship, and where to find the supplies they needed.

After the water boiled, Alexa prepared the coffee by dumping it directly into the pot and then straining it through a cloth. Rusty rinsed out some cups he discovered in the trunk, and they discussed more of his questions about life in the last few millennia over the warm drink.

A small stirring in the leaves beside the stream startled the three as Lucky popped out of the undergrowth with a quail in her mouth. They were impressed at the pig's resourcefulness. Alexa pet her behind the ears as she snatched the quail and threw it over to John to prep it for cooking.

"It's time for me to go," Rusty suggested, as he stood and passed his cup to Alexa.

Grabbing his hand, she pulled him close and kissed him sweetly on the cheek.

With a wink, he turned to the western path leading toward the cruise ship. He snatched up a new satchel, placed his machete and knife inside, and brought out his last pineapple and tossed it to John.

John caught the fruit. "Thanks! Are you sure you don't want to wait a moment for the quail to cook?"

"I'll try to be resourceful along my journey." Rusty nodded and called to Lucky to join him.

With a quick snap of the wrist, John tossed a piece of the quail, which Lucky quickly gobbled up, and they were on their way.

Rusty hoped it wouldn't be too much longer before the path to the waterfall connected with the one they were on. After fifteen minutes of walking, he came to a rope bridge that crossed the chasm. It thrashed back and forth, and there was no way Lucky would possibly make it across. It was made of three ropes: two for holding on to and the third to walk. The ropes were tied together with a zigzag pattern that linked them to the footpath. It was dangerous and Rusty considered leaving Lucky to make the journey.

"It looks as if your journey is done. You should go back to John and Alexa," Rusty suggested. He braced himself and started down the bridge. Lucky curled up at the entrance and refused to leave even as Rusty tried to coax her away. The bridge was sturdy at first, but as he made his way to the middle, it jerked under the strain of his weight. He looked down to concentrate on each foot placement on the thick rope beneath him. Rusty's feet blurred as he focused on the depths below. With the thought of falling into the ravine, his body trembled.

Branches released from the trees ahead and flew past him as the storm gained strength. As the rain set in, he urged himself forward and stepped carefully. The rope immediately became slick and his foot slipped. His left leg fell off the center line, and he grasped at the ropes on the side to steady himself. Tangled in the wet ropes, he fell on the bridge.

Lucky screeched out, circling back and forth at the entrance, as Rusty held on for his life.

He grasped on tightly to the side rope as the bridge rippled in the currents. Gradually, he pulled himself off the center rope, got to a kneeling position, and reached up for the hand rope.

Suddenly, the bridge jerked as the ropes snapped, knocking him off the side. The clasp on his boot snagged on the bottom rope and suspended him upside down from the bridge. He reached up with all his might to grab the bottom rope, but his boot began to slip off his foot.

He flexed his foot to stop it from sliding out and sending him down to his death. As he hung upside down, he wrapped his right foot around the snagged left boot to help it from falling off.

He swayed with the bridge, gathering his energy for another thrust upward. As the bridge moved up to the peak of its ark, he lunged forward with all his momentum and grasped the footrope with his hand. His foot slipped out of the boot at the exact moment he managed to get his second hand on the rope. He waited for the bridge to swing back so he could get up on top of it. The rope again met its pinnacle in the swing, and he used its momentum to pull himself up to his belly and wrap his arm around the zigzagged side rope.

Thunder boomed in the distance. The rain increased, leaving him soaked and exposed on the bridge. The side clasp of his boot remained intertwined in the rope. He didn't dare use two hands, as he reached down for the boot, but it wouldn't budge. It would have to stay. After giving up, he rocked in the momentum as he regained a standing position, and moved forward toward the other side.

He heard a snapping sound unlike the normal bridge creaks as it swayed. Rusty looked up from his feet to the end of the bridge. A man was cutting away the handhold to the bridge! The same man who stabbed John. The man called Bobby!

Adrenaline shot through his body, and Rusty turned and started back toward Lucky. The pig squealed and circled back and forth near the entrance to the bridge, unable to do anything for him. She screeched again as the first rope snapped and nearly sent Rusty plummeting to the bottom of the canyon.

He regained his balance, leaning left as the right rope fell slack. Turning quickly, he cursed himself for turning around. He would not make it at this rate.

Seconds later, Bobby cut through the second handhold, again sending Rusty off balance. He fell to the foot rope, grasping on for dear life. His momentum swung him under the rope and he held on with both hands. He gained his composure and wrapped his legs around the last rope.

The sides of the rope tangled him up as he tried to hurry to the side where Lucky frantically scampered. Vibrations shook the line as man thrashed at the last rope with his knife. Three-quarters of the way there, Rusty tangled his arms in the rope. His heart nearly leaped out of his chest. An instant later, a snapping sound filled Rusty's ears.

§§§

The bridge flew down like a rope swing and smashed up against the side of the gorge. The man with the machete grunted as he slammed into the granite wall, and the sounds of bones cracking echoed through the gorge.

"Shut up!" Bobby screamed as he tossed a rock across the gorge at the screeching boar. It fell short. Bobby panted, mumbling something incoherent as he searched for another rock. He grasped at a slightly larger stone and felt its weight. Bobby cursed again as he hurled it at the boar. The stone sailed across the opening with precision, hitting the pig just above the right ear. The animal yelped in pain, lost its balance and hit the dirt. The boar then stood back up on all fours and bolted up the path.

"I will kill them," Bobby chanted, as he hurled stones at the limp man tangled in the bridge. Over and over the man's body shook as it was pounded by Bobby's rocks. A gust surged through the gorge as if to say it was over. It stretched the bridge and forced the ropes high up the side of the wall releasing the tangled man. The pummeled, broken body fell downward, spiraling off the granite walls like a rag doll, head over heels until he crashed into the floor of the gorge below. Bobby cheered as the man's body was surely crushed on impact.

No one could survive that fall.

CHAPTER 17

Damp and shivering, Alexa and John sat huddled in the bed as wind and rain pelted the cabin. Lucky scrambled into the house in a flurry, howling and snorting and sending the two into a panic. She was bleeding!

"Where's Rusty?" Alexa yelled to Lucky, as the pig tore out into the rain.

Her father threw a blanket tightly over her shoulders, pulling her back into the cabin trying to calm her. But nothing could stop her from scrambling with worry for this man, whom they had just met, yet who made such an impression on her, who saved her father's life.

"Where is he, little girl?" John yelled over his shoulder as he limped to the doorway.

The pig responded by running toward the path, snorting

and looking back at them.

"Dad, he must be in trouble. I have to go help him." Alexa pleaded.

"It is too dangerous, Alexa. Wait 'til it dies down."

"I can't, Dad. I need to help him and you need medicine," Alexa begged and John reached for her arm, but she pulled away. She dug into a chest for some better-fitting clothes, considering the weather, and she tossed garments over her shoulder as she assessed each item. Close to the bottom, out came a rain slicker, and she held it outstretched and measuring it up. It was far too big for her small frame, but she put it on as she fled the cabin.

"I'll be back soon, Dad. I love you," she called back to him where he stood in the doorway.

Lucky tore down the path, and Alexa scampered through the mud trying to keep up, but there was no way of matching pace with a boar in her element. Almost instantly the rain and wind stopped, leaving a gloomy haze that blanketed the island. Alexa struggled to keep Lucky in view as she sprinted down the path. Her feet sank down into the mud, pulling her shoes off. She hopped on one leg to adjust her shoe and landed it back down into a full sprint.

After a few minutes, Lucky stopped at a lookout point, circling and snorting wildly at a strange structure—three posts overlooking the gorge. She stepped close to the edge and realized it was a fallen rope bridge. As she glanced wearily over the edge down the granite wall to the jungle below, her stomach turning from the dizzying height.

The bridge, shifting in the gorge, held something dangling from it. Reaching down she struggled to pull up the heavy, rain-soaked ropes. Her shoulders and arms burned from the exertion, but she was determined. One foot at a time, she used all her weight to fall backward and drag more of the bridge up to her side of the gorge.

Resting for a moment, she took deep breaths. Her eyebrows tensed and she gritted her teeth as she reached down and fell back one last time. The object finally popped over the side. A boot. Rusty's boot!

She screamed and let go and the rope bridge tumbled back down over the edge. The image of Rusty falling from the bridge to the depths below filled her mind. *No one could survive that fall.* Tears poured out as she crawled to the edge to look over, afraid she would find his broken body at the bottom.

From this height, she could barely see the water because the dense growth of tropical plants grew high and thick. She looked down at the wall adjacent to the boot. Massive amounts of blood streaked the side of the granite wall.

Alexa sat back in the mud, crying frantically. Lucky nudged up against her and she embraced the swine with both her arms. She rocked back and forth, trying to come up with a story that made sense that didn't result in losing Rusty. She convulsed as she looked down again over the edge and tried to call out to Rusty, but no words came. She was too choked up to speak.

After a few minutes, her heaving and choking subsided as Lucky rubbed against her side and snorted, displaying love in her eyes. Alexa looked back at the boar and regained her composure, replacing her devastation with determination. *I refuse to lose them both.* She needed to get medicine for her father's leg and nothing would stop her now.

Lucky guided the way along the ridge of the gorge, as Alexa picked up the pace in search of the much-needed supplies. The sun gradually broke through the haze and shown down on her face as she looked to the sky. Her legs were soggy from trudging through the mud, and her shoes squished with every step.

As the sun poked through, the heat intensified inside her rain coat, and she took it off. Resting with her back against a tree, she removed her soggy pants and tossed them and the raincoat over her shoulder.

After a short time, she made her way to a second footbridge. Two strong ropes provided sturdy handholds, and the bottom was crafted of boards measuring three-feet wide. With a successful hop on the first few boards, she realized it was safe enough to pass, and she and Rusty's boar carefully crossed the chasm.

Once Alexa made it to the other side, she hit the ground running with new purpose and drive. Her hair lifted in the wind of her wake as she cruised across the rocky ground and closed in on the shore. After half an hour, the jungle opened up to the beach. Ships, new and old, were on display in varying levels of decay. She recalled the conversation with Rusty as he had described the immense destruction.

She rested for a moment in the sun with Lucky and decided to hang up the rain gear and her pants to dry as she made her way down the beach. Far off in the distance, the cruise ship still stood, giving her hope. She jogged, kicking up sand with Lucky at her side.

Lucky remained focused and hadn't uttered a sound. From their first meeting, Lucky showed courage, compassion, and determination. She admired the little animal and vowed to herself that she would always take care of Lucky.

Alexa placed her hands on her knees and caught her breath as she faced the bow of the ship, contemplating the easiest way to board the vessel. Looking up at a thick rope that hung down from somewhere inside the bow, she thought of climbing it. That would be a difficult task. Alexa moved to the side of the boat and looked down the edge to where the deck of the boat was level with the ocean. Removing her shoes, she stepped into the warm, comfortable sea. Just when she was about to jump in to swim, something caught her eye. A shimmer in the waves stopped her in her tracks. Hundreds of jellyfish.

With a quick jump, she grabbed on to the rope with both hands, wrapped her legs around it, and made her way up. It was a grueling climb, and she thought of her high school physical education class with each tug.

Each year, standards were set in climbing the rope, pushups, sit-ups, pull-ups, and running to meet the federation's minimum requirements. She was fortunate to grow up on Earth, rather than in the space stations, where she would have been preserved in stasis. After years of being frozen, the generations never woke up quite the same. Their muscles and minds were fatigued. She recalled the stories her father told her of his awakening. For six months, he had to regain his muscle strength before making the voyage back to the reformed island of Australia.

At the top of her ascent, Alexa climbed over the railing and inspected the deck. Without her shoes, the steep floor was slick, and she pursed her lips as she looked over the railing at her shoes, still sitting where she'd left them.

Choking and retching over the stench of rotting human bodies, she doubled over and covered her face while holding tightly to the railing. Trying desperately not to breathe through her nose, Alexa recalled her checklist of things they needed. Food, antibiotics, a stitch kit, and bandages, with second priorities being a new set of boots and possibly a change of clothes.

She traveled down the deck, hand over hand, grasping the railing tightly as her feet slipped on the slimy wood. Standing parallel to the stairwell leading downstairs, she contemplated trying to scurry across the deck, but it was too dangerous. She got an idea and traveled back up and grasped the rope that led to the shoreline. Pulling it up, she tossed the length down the center of the deck, but it fell short of the stairwell by fifteen feet.

Inching her way down the slanted deck, she reached the end of the rope. She let go, slid down into the stairwell, and thumped down three stairs before she could snag the railing and stop her decent. Suffering a bashed elbow and hip, she rubbed them with her free hand and winced at the pain. She'll surely have a nasty bruise in a few hours.

Favoring her hip as she traveled down the stairs, she passed the first and second floors. As she entered the hallway lined with cabins, the light drifted into blackness. She wearily looked down the hall. With a breath of relief, Alexa spotted her cabin. She reached out and grasped the handle of the door marked 325. It was locked.

She cursed as she shook the door and banged her fist repeatedly on the wall in frustration. Since it was a ship, and ships lose power, they not only offered keycards or handprint access, but each door contained a manual lock as well. This meant there was a master key, but where would that be? Janitorial staff would have it and maybe the customer service desks or housekeeping.

Housekeeping! She passed her room and down the side hall and found the housekeeping office with the door wide open. Inside the room was pitch black, as the rays of light were completely filtered out, and the stench was horrible. Completely blind, she felt her way along the wall, not knowing what was in store for her. She slipped on a towel, landed on her butt hard, and slid into the room, smashing up against a clothes dryer. Standing, she gained her balance, feeling with outstretched arms, looking for something that would hold a key.

Again, she tripped over something and fell, but this time the object was soft. Covering her mouth, she gagged. It was one of the housekeepers. Tears soaked Alexa's face as she felt up and down the sides of the body. The woman was soaking wet and sticky. Alexa was sure it was blood, guts, or something else equally disgusting. She held her hand to her mouth and convulsed, trying to hold herself back from puking. As she felt down to the woman's waist, the sweet jingling sound of keys echoed in the room. She snatched the key ring and tried to stand while still heaving.

Alexa tried her best to walk up the slant to the top of the room where the entrance was, but she slipped back, and with nothing to hold onto, she couldn't find a way out of the room. She crouched back down to the ground and tried it on all fours, but the ground was also covered in the same gross liquid. As she put her hands down into it, she could no longer hold back and dry heaved.

She laid over on her back and attempted to push herself backward up and out of the room like a crab. Feeling first for wetness, and then placing her hand down, she progressed toward the doorway. Once out of the room, she gasped for air and stood in the slanted hallway, gathering her energy.

Back at her room, she tried several keys and finally heard a click with the right key. As she opened the door, the light from the porthole shined into the hallway, and it slightly blinded her. After a moment, her eyes adjusted and she searched the room. She'd expected a mess, but not this bad. The interior room had stayed dry, but her suitcase had exploded, and the table, beds, and chairs were all jammed up against the wall. She sifted through the furniture and found her father's suitcase and backpack. She opened the pack and found a flashlight, a medical kit, and a knife. This was his military-issued backpack.

"Yes!" she called out elated. "Dad, why didn't you say anything about this?"

Alexa fished through the rest of her clothes. She grabbed a swimsuit and a few pair of panties, two bras, a pair of shorts, one sarong, and her favorite hoodie, and she jammed them into the pack.

"Tampons! I need tampons," she muttered as she rifled through the wreckage of her room. She cried out as she hugged the box, still dry. Back to her mental list, she found some pants and her boots. Alexa thought it was strange at first when her dad insisted she needed to bring boots. *He's going to laugh at me. He was right, as usual.*

For her father, she grabbed a pair of pants, a few shirts and boxers, sandals, socks, and now the backpack was full. As she threw the backpack around her and tightened the straps, she removed and replaced her panties and covered up with a pair of shorts. On second thought, she took the backpack off and changed her bra and shirt and strapped it back on. With antibiotics and food on her mind, she left the room.

She entered the hallway and checked the medical box on the wall. It had some dry bandages, a silver blanket, gauze, tape, and small tubes of antibiotic ointment. She stuffed what she found into the backpack, and checked a second box in the other main hallway on that floor.

Now all that was left was food. Alexa tried to recall the dining and kitchen area of the ship. She looked down the hallway that sank into the sea, and determined that it would have to be toward the bow.

Holding on to the side railing, she gradually made her way up to the front of the ship. She'd guessed correctly and found the kitchen that catered to guests on this level of the ship. She searched for things that would be easy to prepare, but also nonperishable. Alexa found what she was looking for in the dry pantry. This fifty by fifty foot room was packed with baking ingredients, grains, and pasta, and so much more.

With her backpack half-full, she settled on several bags of pasta, jars of marinara, rice and beans, and a few canned vegetables. That would get their strength up. She also grabbed a canister of oats with dried berries. Before leaving the kitchen, she took the chance of opening the freezer. As she had guessed, it was easily seventy degrees Fahrenheit and everything was spoiled. She held her nose as the rancid stench quickly filled the kitchen, and she hurried to close the large door.

Armed with necessities, she headed back to the top of the ship and clawed her way to the bow. As she stood up and looked over the railing, her jaw dropped at the sight of a man on the shore chasing Lucky with a knife.

CHAPTER 18

Lucky tore across the sand just out of reach of the man who had stabbed her father. Alexa remembered him from the night of the storm. His friends had called him Bobby. She ducked back down. She was trapped, for if she tried to throw the rope over, she would be seen trying to descend. Lucky was in no threat, as she was at least triple the speed as the attacker, but Alexa, with a heavy pack, would be easy to catch.

With her hands to her head she wracked her brain for ideas on how to gain distance from the man. She couldn't leave Lucky, so she ruled out sneaking back to the path immediately. How could she get her and the boar back up the hill and leave the crazy person behind? Even if she gained distance, he would surely follow her. She needed to be fast.

Lifeboat! She rappelled down the side of the cruise liner and located a lifeboat still intact just above the water, attached to the side around the second deck. She hurried down the side of the boat, holding the railing and made it to the deck just above the launch.

Checking the shoreline for Bobby, she lifted herself over the edge, climbed down to the second level, and threw her backpack into the boat. As she unlocked the latch and lowered the boat to the water with the hand crank, a large clank rung out. She set the boat adrift, hopped in, and checked the gas gauge. It was ready to go.

Bobby came back into sight, still trudging through the sand after Lucky. She had to think carefully about how to get the pig.

As she fired up the engine, both Lucky and Bobby's attention shifted to the sudden noise. She pulled away from the ship, heading eastward, and Lucky tore off toward the boat, gaining significant ground from Bobby. She traveled down the shoreline until she was sure she was out of range from Bobby and pulled up to the sand, careful not to bury the hull on the beach. Hopping out, she called to Lucky, who sprinted toward her with Bobby still chasing her.

As Lucky got closer, she realized Lucky wasn't running toward her but off to the side and further down the beach. Alexa followed the line Lucky traveled and spotted something off in the distance. As the pig passed her, Alexa squinted to see what was in the sand, which was difficult in the sun light reflecting off the island.

As Lucky decreased the distance between her and the object, Alexa followed the boar in the boat. Bobby was at least a quarter mile back but still trying to catch up. Nearing Lucky's destination, she realized what the boar was after. A man lay face down in sand. Rusty!

Quickly, she popped the boat back into gear and sped as close to Rusty as possible. She hopped out and sprinted toward him. Blood was splattered everywhere, and he wasn't moving. Alexa slid down to him and turned him over in a panic. He was breathing, but wouldn't wake up.

"Rusty, wake up!" she screamed, as the attacker gained ground. Dragging him by his hands in the sand slowly, she screamed his name over and over, pleading for him to wake up. Her shoulders and legs flexed under the strain of his weight. Foot after foot, she made it to the shoreline. Reaching down, she hoisted Lucky into the boat. She could hear the loud chants from the frantic man as he gained ground.

"I will kill them!" he screamed from only a few hundred yards away.

Alexa panted and heaved as she tried lifting Rusty, but he was simply too heavy.

"Rusty, please wake up," she pleaded and slapped him in the face.

When she reached for the white bumper still hanging over the side, she caught a glimpse of the man with the knife. He was now within a hundred yards of them. She unhooked it from the rope and quickly knotted a slipknot. Tying it over Rusty's hand, she yanked it tight and climbed over the side of the boat as the killer reached them.

Bobby thrust himself at Alexa and grabbed her left foot.

Turning over to face the attacker, she stretched for

the glove compartment by the steering wheel. The man emerged from the water and threw his leg over the side of the boat. She popped the lock on the compartment and reached in for the flare gun. It wasn't there. But she did grab hold of an air horn.

He placed one foot over the edge, and Lucky lunged toward him, growling and snapping. The man kicked at Lucky as they faced off, and Alexa pressed down on the trigger of the air horn right in his face. He reached for his ears, and she hit him square in the jaw with a mean left hook.

He flew off the boat and landed on Rusty. She threw the boat in gear and watched over the side as she pulled away from the shore. As she gained distance from the attacker, she watched Rusty's body, still dangling from the rope as the waves pushed him under.

Bobby, with a knife in his teeth, swam and yelled at the boat.

A few hundred yards away from him, she reached over and down under Rusty's armpits. With all her might, she stood and fell backward to lift Rusty into the boat. They both came crashing down onto the deck with Rusty on top of her. She rolled him over, moving out from underneath him.

He woke.

"Rusty? Oh, Rusty, you're okay? I can't believe this! I thought you were dead. I thought I lost you forever." She kissed his face over and over.

He wearily tried to sit up, but he couldn't. Lucky hopped on his chest with her front two hooves and licked him in the face.

"That man tried to kill me. The man who stabbed your father," Rusty muttered, trying to steady himself.

"Just stay down. We have to go," she said as she stepped to the captain's chair and dropped the boat into gear. They took off fast and left the crazy man in their wake as they headed past the southernmost tip of the island, toward the obelisk.

Rusty gathered his strength and sat up. Then he dragged and pulled his way to the chair beside Alexa.

She lessened up on the throttle to an even cruising speed and reached out to hold his hand.

"Where are we? What's happening?" he asked.

"You left to get supplies for Dad, and Lucky came back bleeding and in a panic. I took off after her and she stopped at the bridge. Your boot was attached to the side of the of the fallen bridge, but you were nowhere to be found." She fought back tears. "I thought you were dead."

"I think I was," Rusty confirmed.

"I don't understand."

"Neither do I. The last thing I remember was trying to get back to Lucky. That man was cutting the ropes to the bridge, so I turned back and tried to make it back to the side. When the bridge snapped, I went crashing toward the wall. Then all went black, and I woke up here."

"There was blood all over the wall. You must have fallen! No one could survive that fall." Alexa cried out and hugged Rusty.

"That explains how I woke up on the beach earlier, as well. I must have died then, too." Rusty stopped a moment. "That doesn't explain why I can remember now, though." He drew his brows together as he watched Alexa drive the boat. "How are you doing that?"

"It's a power boat," Alexa said. "Here, let me show you." She idled the throttle, and the water calmed behind the boat. She stepped off the chair and walked back to Rusty's side. She pointed out the propeller and explained the system up to the throttle and steering wheel. With the last statement, she took Rusty's hand and guided him to the chair and urged him to try. He took the throttle and eased it a bit. The boat took off and produced the largest smile Alexa had ever seen from him. She crouched behind him and wrapped her left hand around his chest, placed her right hand on his and pulled the throttle all the way.

For the moment, her pain and confusion was replaced with the exhilaration of the ride and the joy of finding Rusty alive. With her arms wrapped around his chest, she held on tightly to this man, this enigma.

He turned his head to meet her gaze and kissed her cheek.

Alexa couldn't help but cry. The mere thought of losing Rusty had been devastating.

All the recent events pushed her far outside her comfort zone. With the death of her mother not long ago, she had teetered on the edge of a breakdown. This time with Rusty had helped her so much. It showed her the possibility of love. He was a man with strength, who was brave and kind. She let herself cry and held him tightly as they passed the obelisk.

With her hand on his, she adjusted the throttle. He pointed the boat to the path's entrance. At the last moment, she reversed the thrust and slowed the small craft down so it eased into the shore. Rusty commented on her adept skills as he tossed over the anchor. Lucky launched off the back of the boat with a belly flop, splashing them both. They let out a laugh at the sight of Lucky and Rusty hopped over the bow to land. Alexa tossed him the pack and she jumped out of the boat.

Hand in hand, they walked up the trail to Rusty's cabin. They talked about Rusty's struggle with the man on the bridge and contemplated how he ended up on the beach. Something was missing. Something about Rusty or this place. Something that was protecting him. Rusty pointed out how fast the man got to the other side of the bridge, as well. That meant there was a shortcut.

"There must be another path to the north that cuts across the island. The place where the darkened beings were. The top of the heart," Rusty commented, as he pointed north.

"Yes, I bet there's some other trail that leads to the gorge, or the other side of it starting over there," Alexa pointed to the west.

"Or maybe he snuck by us in the night," Rusty suggested.

"Nope, the monkeys or Lucky would have alerted us as soon as he got close."

"I remember the monkeys, as I followed Bobby and Sergio, the day I met you. I believe you're correct, which leaves only the north as a possibility."

"Then again, the distance from the beach to the bridge where you fell . . . where I found your boot . . . is so far. You got there in a matter of just a few hours."

"Originally, I woke up in that same spot with no memory. This time, I didn't lose my recent memory of what happened before I died. I remember you and John, Lucky, my cabin…"

241

"That certainly alludes to something more significant at the first awakening. Something must have happened that was much more serious."

"Something more serious than death?" Rusty asked.

"Something more serious than death." Alexa nodded.

"There's still not enough information to draw any sort of conclusion," Rusty said.

"I know," she replied. "But what are we missing?"

"Are there any technologies in your era that could revive the dead?" Rusty asked.

"Not that I know of. But I bet people have been trying to accomplish that since your time." Alexa walked up the muddy path, together with Rusty.

"Wait, you said there were terraformers spread across the planet, and they basically wiped out everything that was and brought it back to a pristine state." Rusty remembered the technologies they had discussed.

"Yes, why do you ask?"

"You said that essentially it would have killed any human in proximity, including me, but since I evidently don't have any death issue, that doesn't matter I suppose, but you see the boats and the other crafts on the shore. Nothing has destroyed them."

"You're right! This entire place has not been terraformed," she concluded out loud.

"I think the bigger question is, why wasn't it terraformed? Was it by accident, or on purpose?"

"I doubt it was by accident. It must be one of the two anomalies from the story of the necklace. "

"I agree, but why didn't the people try to fix the issue by sending more crews down?" he asked, trying to piece everything together.

"I am not entirely sure. You'll have to ask my dad. I remember that he mentioned it was no longer profitable to fix the glitch."

"Money," Rusty stated matter-of-factly. "I figured that by now, people would have figured out a better way to live."

"For a short time, money went away when people remained in orbit of the planet. Originally, they had such limited resources that they imposed a ration system. That eventually turned to trade, and money was reborn."

The troop of monkeys cried out warnings which were repeated up the jungle. As soon as Rusty and Alexa entered the first clearing, Alexa noticed something was wrong.

"Rusty," she said quietly.

"Yes?"

"Where's the body of Bobby's friend? It's gone."

Rusty looked around the area, then grabbed her hand and quickened their pace to Rusty's cabin.

"Dad!" Alexa called out, but he didn't reply. They ran toward the house.

"Welcome back, you two. What's the rush?" John happily greeted them with Lucky already on his lap, looking for attention. "Oh, especially you, little Lucky," John chuckled at the boar and gave her a rub down.

"Dad, we called to you and you didn't answer! What is all this?" Alexa gestured toward the three open trunks.

"I was keeping myself busy. Rusty, I hope you don't mind me going through your things."

"Please do. Maybe you can teach me about myself

from what you find."

"I believe I can," John said.

Rusty smiled. "What's really important is how your leg is healing."

"Honestly, it is not too great. I believe it's getting infected. On the bright side, it's not bleeding," John acknowledged, as he reached down to take off the wrap.

"I bet we need to give it a stitch or two anyway. Let's look, Dad." Alexa knelt and helped unwrap the dressing. "Yeah, it's not good. Let's get it washed up first, then you can teach me how to do stitches." Alexa picked up his crutches and led him to the stream. John sat on the edge and gave his leg a good washing as Alexa sorted through the backpack.

"Oh, my pack. I love you. I guess you made it to our room on the ship," John said with a big smile.

"And I found tampons!" She lifted the box over her head, as if brandishing a trophy.

"No kidding! That's the number one answer to the question 'If I were ever stranded on a deserted island with only one item to bring . . .' Well . . . at least that's the answer for the ladies."

She burst out laughing.

"What are tampons?" Rusty asked.

Alexa forgot their audience in her excitement. Her face reddened and she quickly put the box away.

"It's a lady thing. Honey, did you find the stitch kit?" John quickly changed the subject.

"Here we go," Alexa called out as she pulled the kit from the bag and handed it to John.

Both Rusty and Alexa watched carefully as John showed them both a square knot a few times, and then they washed their hands in the river and each tried a few themselves. In total, John's leg got twelve stitches and he gritted his teeth tightly through each one.

After applying plenty of antibiotic ointment, Alexa handed Rusty the tape as she cut off some gauze and placed it on the wound.

"What is this? It's great." Rusty pulled off a piece.

"Tape," John chuckled. "There are so many things we take for granted, my friend. By the way, what happened to you? Lucky came back all bloodied up after you left, and we were worried that you were dead."

Rusty froze. Alexa could feel his uncertainty in not knowing how to answer her dad's question and snagged the tape from him to finish the job. "Dad, what did you uncover?" she asked instead.

"Some clothes, mac and cheese, thousand-year-old trinkets, a tunnel and the secrets in Rusty's past," John said with a grin, apparently trying to be funny.

"What is mac and cheese?" Rusty raised an eyebrow.

Alexa attempted to focus on the important facts. "Food, Rusty." She turned to her father. "And Dad, cut it out. You found a tunnel? Seriously?"

"Yes, it's under the porch over there. It seems our friend here has been looking for clues of his past for a long time, and the answer is somewhere in this island. Oh, and I found Rusty's journal."

CHAPTER 19

"John, with all due respect, I'm not really sure I want to know about my past," Rusty said.

"Why wouldn't you want to know?" Alexa asked.

Rusty removed his shirt and turned his back toward them so they could get a closer look. Thousands of scars riddled his flesh.

"Oh my, I understand," John said. "Remembering your past may uncover some tragedies, but it'll also show your personal triumphs and mistakes. Then you can choose to repeat the ones you want. Understanding yourself is the single most important key to unlocking a full life." John looked at Rusty in earnest.

"I understand what you're saying. We can read a little and I will stop you if it's too much." Rusty said quietly.

John recalled the sections of the highest importance, which he'd bookmarked with leaves when Alexa and Rusty were away.

"Let me begin at the beginning of the journal." John smirked at the play on words.

'"1711 the ship set sail for the Archipelago Islands of the south this morning. There had been rumors that local ships would avoid this area because of fear. King Louis XIV insisted that his reports concluded it was a magical place. The crew has mixed feelings about the adventure, for some have the idea that death surrounds our destination.'

"He goes on about the journey which lasted months. As they get closer, mutiny starts amongst the crew. It was at this point that the storm hit. Very similar in description to the storm we witnessed on the cruise." John nodded to Alexa, and continued. "There are more islands."

John flipped a few more pages and continued with a second excerpt.

'"Within thirty days, the entire crew has perished. Now it is just me! Some died when the storm took the ship, and some even died swimming to the island. Others, like me, were wounded and their injuries became rank. The worst of times occurred when power struggles erupted while the men fought for leadership. Three times over, fights broke out and men were killed for power. It ended with Jacques and Pascal, who killed each other over some local fruit. There was plenty of fruit to go around, but they believed that they had done more work to deserve the first bite. The struggle ended with a machete in Pascal's gut and a dagger in Jacques throat. I sat for hours by their bodies in disbelief of what had just happened. I'm going to continue finishing my cabin at the top of the western mountain and searching for the sound we had been hearing in the night.'"

"What sound?" Rusty interjected.

"It was the first mention of this sound," John replied. "I skimmed the beginning twice, but I suppose I could have missed a first recollection. Don't worry. You explain what it was later."

Alexa opened her mouth to speak, but John held up

his hand. "All in good time, dear." He cleared his throat and continued.

'"With the house in order, I decided to set out on a journey to the shoreline. It seems as if each storm has produced more people to this island. Each group of people pose threats to my existence and way of life. I have made mistakes on several occasions to trust the newcomers, only to end up at the point of a sword. I can't say if they came here as evil, but they certainly changed into evil as they lived here longer. I would prefer to have some companionship, but the last person I knew and trusted died years ago.

"There seems to be some foul play at work on this island, and I truly believe there is no escape. I've watched and almost felt guilty, as I've seen people try to escape, only to end up destroyed on the reef or never making it past the draw to the shores. I believe the island consumes anything that is in its reach. Generations of sea-worthy ships now litter the shores with no hope to return to a life at sea. For me, there is an endless supply of wreckage to plunder if I am careful not to allow my presence to be known.'

"This is where it starts getting good," John added with a grin.

'"I have died on several occasions, and I'm not entirely sure how or why I still end up here. The only thing I am sure of is there is a pool that I drank from that I believe has given me this power of life. Because of this everlasting state, I've been killed or tortured for months by several groups of people and even sometimes more than once. For lifetimes, I've been unable to write my memories, and the truth is, I would rather forget.

'"I recall one group of people who kept me tied up. They beat me each day and starved me to death. When they captured me a second time, they realized I had discovered something bringing me back alive. They tortured me over and over in hopes to find these magical waters. I would never let them know. If I gave them 'the life,' I would be forced to be with these monsters forever. I waited till the last one died of old age before I escaped.'"

John paused as his last words hung in the silence, and Alexa sat with a horrified look on her face.

"I'm so sorry, Rusty," Alexa said. "I hardly know what to say. You've spent a lifetime or more of torture, awaiting your captors' deaths." She grasped his hand and gave him a huge hug.

"It's okay. I'm hearing my own writings, yet I still can't remember. I feel for that man, but I am no longer him. Now, I am more concerned with losing you two. It seems as if I rarely find anyone to pass the time with and think it may be wise to find this source of water for both of you," Rusty suggested.

"The thought of everlasting life is intriguing when you're a child, but in reality, it's incredibly depressing at times. It's hard enough living one life without getting too bored." John chuckled.

Alexa gave her dad a playful shove and a smiled at Rusty. "I'm honored that you would share that with me. I accept!" Alexa grinned and looked over at John.

His smile changed to a frown and his eyes moved off into the distance. Perhaps he was thinking of her mom, Janice.

"It's okay, Dad. I understand."

"I can't say I would consider it. I would rather have the chance at being with my love once more." John sighed and flipped to the next section which he'd marked with a leaf. "'I'm not sure how long it's been since I've written in my journal. There's something on this island that's making me forget. I've obviously been here before, but I don't recall who or what I am. Only these words remind me of the world and the lives I have lived. How many times have I read this?'"

As the last words ran off John's tongue, tears welled up in Rusty's eyes. "Please stop," he said, as he became choked up.

Alexa wrapped her arms around him.

"There's someone else here. Someone like you, but this man is not good. We need to know, Rusty. *You* need to know," John said forcefully.

"I was afraid you'd say that. Do you think he found

the water?" Alexa worried.

"He made the water and protects it," John clarified. "It seems you shouldn't have drunk it. At least he didn't want you to."

"Who protects the waters?" Alexa asked.

"I haven't seen a name mentioned, but it seems as if he's hunting Rusty and using people who land here to try to kill Rusty. Each attempt seems more and more mystical and extreme. He's trying to live and can't with Rusty around."

"Dad, is he dead . . . or does he still have control in this world?"

"Yes, dear. He seems to take forms of people who have died, and Rusty described him as a vague figure on a few occasions. Here, let me continue by reading this next section." John paused and looked to Rusty for his acknowledgement.

With a nod, Rusty wiped his tears and motioned for John to continue.

'"This may or may not be my first encounter with this figure. I'm just not sure. After I killed that angry captain, he came back to life and held my head under water until I died as well. Fortunately, for me, I ended up in the sand far on the other side of the island away from him. He was unable to take my memory this time.'"

"That's probably the same place where I found you, Rusty," Alexa remarked, recalling finding his body on the beach by the cruise liner earlier. Rusty nodded and John continued.

'"My swine companion, Lucky,'" John continued, "'led me back to my home from the shore today. I'm so thankful for her. I've decided that I'm going to find out how to destroy this figure, and I believe that the tunnels under my house must hold the key. Each day I vow to explore more of the catacombs in hopes that, one day, I can live a life of peace."

Lucky had stirred at the sound of her name.

"How many times have I named you Lucky?" Rusty greeted his longtime companion with a huge grin spanning from ear to ear.

Lucky stretched her body after waking and came over to Rusty for some love. She circled his legs and rubbed up next to him with a snort.

John turned the journal sideways and showed the two a map of the recordings Rusty had obviously documented during his travels underground. It was immense and there were no markings related to the pool.

"The good news is, Rusty spent a hundred or so years drawing the caverns underground. A very long time we don't have to repeat. The bad news is the pool is not on the map," John stated.

"Oh, but it is, John. It's right there." Rusty pointed to the center of the heart. "That symbol of a tree is not correct. I did that to acknowledge it was there, yet not let people know if they found the map. The tree is a symbol for life, but there are no trees underground."

"Clever, Rusty," John said.

"All the symbols are above-ground symbols," Rusty said. "We're the only ones who know that it's not on the surface of this island." Rusty suddenly stood up and pointed to the north. Smoke billowed to the clouds.

John and Alexa stood in silence. It was *him*.

"You can hear it," Rusty stated, as Alexa and John

focused intently on the plume. They heard an ominous, grinding sound.

"I'm scared, Dad." Alexa reached out for her father's comfort, but he was entranced at the massive site of the smoke billowing skyward. "What are we going to do?" she asked.

"As you guessed it, it's the sound of *him*," Rusty said. "He's growing in strength. We need to prepare by doing some reconnaissance and finding the pool. We need to know what we're are dealing with and what his weakness are. We need to surprise him by finding out before he knows we're onto him."

John reached out to his daughter and held her tight. "I can't tell you that it's going to be alright. This is beyond anything imaginable."

"It'll be alright, John. He hasn't destroyed me yet." Rusty clenched his fists with determination.

§§§

For the better part of the day, the three prepared to make the journey into the catacombs. John's leg had improved significantly, and he could hobble around, but

Alexa instructed him to rest and take inventory. He sketched out what would be needed for a journey into the depths of the island and crafted a plan for them while Rusty and Alexa did most of the physical work.

Rusty gathered vines, split them, and crafted rope while Alexa found vessels for holding water and gear.

Lucky searched the jungle for birds and brought back two ducks, a pheasant, and a strange looking chicken. The three rested by the small cooking fire John set out. John gradually butchered the birds and hung them to smoke and dry.

"Dad, is there anything in the journal that shows his weaknesses?"

"I haven't seen anything yet, but there must be a way," John replied. "This is my hypothesis. I believe that the terraformers mostly worked, except in certain scenarios that science never uncovered. I recall reports where some of the equipment malfunctioned or just plain went missing. This is one of the locations. The Heart Island anomaly; the same island in the story of the necklace."

Alexa fingered her necklace and shivered as the two

men looked over to her.

Rusty nodded and added, "Are you suggesting we find the missing terraformer and turn it on? That would be extremely dangerous. There's no telling what would happen to us or the island."

John said, "At this point I would not discredit the possibility. Albeit dangerous, it's something he could never be prepared for."

"Unless he is the one that turned it off?" Alexa questioned matter-of-factly. "He also could be using it to draw in more ships. That would explain the violent storms."

"It's possible," John replied. "But that doesn't explain why this phenomenon has existed for hundreds of years. The device has not been in use since the eighteenth century."

"What's left to gather, John?" Rusty asked, eager to get on the move.

"We need lights, boots, socks, a flare gun, and a few more items I have written here, and oh, we need some luck."

"Back to the shore then? I'll get ready." Rusty stood and faced Alexa. "Can you come with me one more time?"

Alexa nodded and looked to her father.

"I'll finish reading," John said. "I guess I should see you both by tomorrow morning. I'll clean this site up and make it look as if no one has been here for a while. I'll hide in the tunnels if I suspect any company."

CHAPTER 20

Alexa and Rusty went west on the path toward their small boat. During their walk, they remained mostly silent. Mixed thoughts flooded Rusty's mind of the recent discoveries, and he was certain she was thinking similar thoughts.

Did she just say she wanted to be with me forever? After all I've been through, what would make her want to stay here forever? How could he be the reason? It must be everlasting life. She must think that it's glorious and romantic. *Now knowing more pieces of my life, I wouldn't want to do it again. Or would I?* He felt a strong connection to this woman. Something more than words could describe. She already saved him from the last attacker. He's already in her debt. Why would she want to risk her life for him? He couldn't imagine anything that he could offer a woman like this.

"I hope no one has taken our boat," she said, finally breaking the silence.

Rusty laughed hard, and it put a smile instantly on her face. "Can you show me how to move it again?" he asked.

"Move it? Oh, the boat. You want me to show you how to drive it." Alexa smiled.

"Yes, drive it. Will you?"

"Yes, I can do that. It's exciting, I know. My dad taught me years ago to drive our boat."

"Evidently, I'm also accustomed to driving a boat, according to your dad's findings."

"Yes, I believe you have. Do you miss it?"

"I don't remember," Rusty said, raising his eyebrow at Alexa.

"I know. I was just kidding," Alexa smiled and placed a kiss on his cheek. Rusty seized the opportunity and put his arms around her before she could back away. His eyes met hers, and the world seemed to fade away into the distance. They stood there for several minutes, gazing at each other.

He was flooded with an explosion of thoughts and feelings. Something so immensely strong, yet calming, swept over him. He bent his head sideways and brushed his lips across hers. She didn't move away, so he pulled her closer and kissed her tenderly and deep. She returned the kiss, and he closed his eyes as his body tingled with delight. He longed for her and never wanted to let her go. Again, they were transported to a cosmic place. This felt so right.

They broke off the kiss softly, remaining in each other's arms.

Alexa opened her eyes and looked at him. "Did you feel that, too?"

"I did. I think I love you," Rusty whispered, shaky at the thought.

"I know. I love you, too," Alexa said softly, as she went in for another kiss.

They met with passion this time and an uncontrollable desire burned inside of Rusty. Her hands gripped his strong shoulders and pulled him closer. Her affection was intense and undeniable. The kiss transported him to a feeling so pure, to a place so beautiful. Bliss.

Lucky snorted and bucked into Alexa's leg.

"Whoa there, little girl! Someone is impatient." Alexa teased the boar.

Rusty realized they needed to get going. He broke the embrace, but his arms ached from the memory of holding her. He breathed deeply. "Come on. We should pick up the pace," he told her, thanks to Lucky's intrusion. Off in the distance, the horizon was black as night. A storm was brewing. Rusty thought they had better be quick to gather supplies and make it back before the storm hit.

Alexa pulled the anchor and Rusty helped her into the boat and he hopped in after her.

They both glanced toward the top of the heart. A small plume of smoke was all that was left as the fuel for the fire had evidently been consumed. They could no longer hear the strange sound.

They looked at each other quickly, and Alexa turned the key, started the engine, pulled the throttle, and headed south. She took Rusty's hand and placed it on the wheel and the other on the throttle. She explained to him how to judge the waves at this speed.

Rusty couldn't help but smile as the boat cruised along the water. He hadn't had this much fun since he woke up from being dead.

The cruise liner came into sight. Something had given way since the last time they'd been there, as the ship was evidently slipping backward into the abyss. It didn't look as if it was safe to board at all, but they badly needed supplies. They discussed the state of the ship and they agreed to stay on top of the main deck to find the things John had asked for. There was no reason to take unnecessary risks. She described in detail the necessities for their journey so he would recognize them.

Alexa guided Rusty as he pulled up against the side of a ship near where the deck met the water, and she threw the anchor. She took two bumpers out and put them over the side to ensure the small boat wouldn't smash too hard into the side of the ship in the waves.

They tightened a knot around the cleat of the ship to their vessel, and then boarded the cruise liner. The big ship creaked as they came onto the deck, and they braced themselves as it shifted. There wasn't much time before the ocean would consume the vessel, and they needed to be cautious and quick.

They shimmied themselves into the room where Rusty had found the first dead body. The odor was now nearly unbearable as the bodies still aboard were well-decomposed. Alexa reached the first-aid box on the wall and told Rusty that was what they were looking for. It was empty, and they agreed to split up to look for others.

Rusty managed his way over to the stairwell and headed down to the first corridor and popped the door on the second first-aid box. He yelled up to Alexa to let her know of his find. She gave a muffled reply, and he made his way back up the stairs to watch her shimmy the boots off a crew member. She gagged repeatedly and Rusty winced at the site.

She looked up at him. "We'll be lucky to find boots. It's a summer cruise ship, so there would be no reason to find anything but sandals and maybe some tennis shoes," she explained. "Oh, I'm sorry. You don't know what sandals or tennis shoes are. It will be forever a mystery to me of what you know and what you don't."

"That's okay. I will learn new things. I did find a crate of—"

The cruise ship suddenly shifted hard and to the port side, throwing them down the deck. Downward they slid, hard and fast, until they plunged into the water above the stern of the ship. The ship finally broke loose of the shore and crept backward into the depths.

"We have to make it to the aft side to free our boat or it will pull it down!" Alexa screamed.

Both frantically swam, dodging wreckage as it broke free around them. A chair came crashing backward, and Rusty dodged it by ducking underwater. As he came up, Alexa wasn't in sight.

"Alexa!" Rusty screamed, and he ducked under the water to see her, but the water was too dark. He didn't believe she could've gone too far from him. With a gasp of breath, he dove down, but he didn't see her. Something grabbed his leg.

Alexa! She was up against the stairwell, reaching for him. Rusty pulled at her arm, but her other hand was lodged between the railing of the stairwell and a table. Surfacing, he took a deep breath and re-submerged. Placed his lips on hers, he gave her the breath. Placing his feet against the wall, he thrust back, trying to pull the table.

Alexa screamed, and bubbles rose from her mouth as the action pinched her forearm.

Rusty met her eyes. Pointing upward, he resurfaced. He took several deep breaths and submerged back toward her. Rusty held her face tightly as he delivered another breath. As he let go, so did the ship, sliding backward and down and away from him. They reached out for each other's hands as they separated. Their fingers touched briefly, and then they were distanced by fathoms.

Rusty quickly surfaced for more air and dove feverishly toward her. He could see Alexa shaking the table back and forth, trying to free her wrist. Further and further down she sank, increasing the distance between her and Rusty. He swam as hard as he could, but he couldn't keep up with the sinking ship. He snagged onto the railing as it passed underneath him and climbed down toward her. As he got closer to her, she heaved, taking in water. He picked up the pace, but he was nearly out of air. Suddenly, the ship's bottom slammed into something sending the bow thrusting forward toward Rusty's back.

He reached and grabbed onto her leg as the ship sunk further and further down. With all his might, he placed his feet on the wall and pulled at the railing until her arm came free, but it was too late, he was out of air. They floated, slightly rising as the ship separated from them, and disappeared below.

And the world went black.

§§§

Rusty woke on the beach, covered in sand. Disoriented, he sat up and tried to think of what was happening. He realized he had died once more. "Alexa!" he belted out, made his way to his feet, and hurried toward the last resting place of the cruise ship. His heart raced and his body ached. His feet thudded and slipped in the sand awkwardly as he pushed himself on. Eventually, he made it back to where the ship used to rest. Now it remained deep below, eaten by the abyss. Rusty fell to his knees.

"Alexa! Alexa!" he screamed, as he sat back on his

heels and covered his face.

A rustling behind him caught his attention, and he turned to see Lucky emerge from out of the jungle. His heart sank because it wasn't his love.

"Rusty! I'm here!" Alexa waved and ran toward him. They met with such force that he took her off her feet and they crashed into the sand. They kissed deeply, and the world swirled around them.

"I thought I lost you," he said, taking a breath, then kissed her again. He held her close to him. "I thought you were dead. What happened?"

"I'm not sure. I woke up floating on my back and you weren't around. I thought you might have died... again."

"As a matter of fact, I did, and you didn't come get me. I was so worried," Rusty told her.

"I had just made it over to the shore and laid down to catch my breath. I must have blacked out again. I heard you calling my name and saw you here," Alexa said, burying her face in his chest.

"I'm just glad you're alive. Are you okay? We really

have to go." Rusty pointed toward the storm front. It was crawling dangerously close to the island.

"We still need supplies. Let's take one last look, quickly," Alexa suggested, and jerked her head to a large vessel not far away.

They stood up from the sand and jogged over to the ship. They hoisted themselves up the ladder to the deck and scooted over to the pilothouse. The door was open and they passed the ship's wheel to a first aid box. Sure enough, it had a flare and a silver blanket which Alexa quickly confiscated.

"We should go to the ship's quarters," Rusty suggested. "I'm sure this place will have some boots and possibly some rope."

Alexa followed Rusty down the stairs to the crew's lounge and the sleeping quarters. The first room offered a nasty corpse, and Rusty immediately shut the door because the old dead guy stunk too much to bear. The second room was clear of the dead and contained plenty of men's clothes and some boots.

Alexa found four yellow rain slickers and a good

bag to stuff them in. With newfound excitement, they split up and quickly made their way through the remaining quarters—thirty rooms in all. They met back in the hallway with two bags filled with rope, clothes, a few knives, and some medical supplies. Alexa also had a bag of things he didn't recognize.

By the time they made it back to the deck, the wind had picked up significantly, and the rain sprinkles became harder by the minute. They each threw over the two bags they had gathered and climbed back down to the beach. Lucky waited eagerly for them and they set up the path to make a semi-direct route to Rusty's cabin.

The rain pelted down on them as they made their way into the jungle. Alexa stopped Rusty, and laid down the bag. She unzipped it and produced a slicker and some boots and handed them to Rusty. She followed suit and removed her sandals and put on a slicker and some boots. She zipped up the bag and tossed the strap back over her shoulder.

"Sorry, Lucky. I didn't find anything for you to keep dry," Alexa apologized to the pig and gave her a good petting.

Lucky let out a whine and kicked her hooves in the mud.

"Oh, poor little piggy," Rusty added, with a frown.

Alexa grabbed Rusty's hand and they headed back up the path. Quickly they passed the pineapple grove and gathered a few in the downpour. It was slick work, making it up the incline, but they trudged on. Soon it became dark and they could only see a few feet ahead of them. They sat down under some large leaves and held each other tight, waiting out the storm. Lucky curled up at their feet covered in one of the dayglow yellow slickers they found on the ship.

Dusk turned into night and the rain eased up.

"We should get going," Alexa suggested. "I have a flashlight."

"A what?" Rusty asked, confused.

"Here, hold this." Alexa offered him a pile of clothes to hold as she dug through the bag with the things he didn't recognize. She pulled out the thing called a flashlight and turned it on. Light suddenly shined from the end and vibrantly illuminated their path.

"Nice trick! Are you a witch?" Rusty laughed out loud.

"Maybe, "Alexa said with a smirk. "One more word out of you, and I'll turn you into something for Lucky to eat," They laughed, replaced the clothes in the bag, zipped it up, and set out back up the path. Hours later, they made it to the foot bridge and on to the camp.

"Dad?" Alexa yelled out, but there was no reply. She entered the shack and searched but there were no signs of John.

"Maybe he is in the tunnel?" Rusty asked. "The storm was pretty heavy. Let's go find out."

They made their way to the bulkhead and lifted it. John wasn't there either.

"Wait, don't move!" Alexa halted Rusty. "There are tracks. Dad said he would clean this place. Look there." She pointed to the entrance leading down to the beach. "You can see Dad swept this place, and yet there are tracks leading into this area."

Rusty carefully avoided the tracks and made his

way over to the entrance.

"I see four distinct tracks leading here. Dad would have seen them coming, and the monkeys would have warned him if they came from this direction. It doesn't make sense."

"There over by the house—three tracks leading in and out. And there's blood," Rusty said, as he pointed.

Both tried to discern what happened from the footprints and the blood pooling up in the mud. The area was muddy from the storm, but it made it easier to see that whoever came for John had definitely ambushed him.

"No, please no!" Alexa yelled out. A body was covered up just beyond the cleared-out area on the far right. She sprinted and fell to the ground, frantically removing leaves from the body. She let out a sigh of relief. It was not her father.

The body lay curled up in a fetal position with a knife in his back. It was a short man with black skin that was peeling off. His eyes remained open, and his pupils reflected red. Nothing about this man seemed natural.

"I thought it was Dad," she said, shaking and crying.

"I think your dad got this one and covered it up. This is one of the beings I had seen before. Why would they go into the dense jungle rather than taking the path?" Rusty asked.

"There must be another path beyond the trees. You can see how the four tracks also come in this direction," Alexa said.

Following the individual trails into the jungle, they discovered that the two paths merged about thirty meters in. They converged and led down a single path to the north.

"I bet this leads to where the fire was," Alexa suggested. "Yes, that means they didn't come all at once. They probably caught him by surprise and from behind. I bet he was waiting here. He just didn't realize there was a path behind him."

"Yes, that makes sense. We need to formulate a plan to get him back." Rusty called to Alexa, who was looking down the trail.

"There! You can see drag marks leading away. He must be alive, but they knocked him out. There's also no blood past this point. Good job, Dad. Please stay alive."

"Let's get what we need together and go down this path," Rusty suggested.

"Maybe we should go down to the beach. I bet they probably wouldn't expect us from that direction," Alexa offered.

"It is a risk because we're not sure that they lead to the same place."

They gathered up some of their dried food and Rusty's journal from the house. Rusty packed them in the bag he'd scavenged from the ship, and they headed down to the beach. Shortly after entering the path, the monkeys sounded the alarm, and the two picked up the pace, with Lucky following close behind.

As the jungle opened to the beach, they sat and ate some dried meat and drank deeply from the canteen Rusty was wearing. They hopped into the boat they had beached earlier and traveled to the northern tip of the island. Hopping off the boat, Alexa darted toward the silver sphere Rusty had witnessed crashing into the shore earlier.

"This is a rescue ship," Alexa said.

"I saw it crash. I checked and the person inside is

dead," Rusty said.

They turned into the top of the heart and followed the river down the gorge. Rusty believed they were close to where the smoke plume had originated. They needed to move more cautiously from this point on. Slowly, they edged their way along the side of the jungle, careful not to be seen.

A short time later, a fire pit lay before them, with a massive circle carved in the sand around the pit, and they spotted a tunnel leading down into the earth. Alexa and Rusty gathered their composure, stripped down to their necessary gear, and stashed the rest of their supplies in the jungle.

Rusty took a deep breath, nodded to Alexa, and led the way into the depths of the island.

CHAPTER 21

Earlier that morning . . .

John watched Alexa and Rusty leave in silence, secretly thinking to himself they should just speak. Time is too short and he of all people should know that. Remembering his love, his wife, his dreams and aspirations, he reminisced of times of happiness and things left undone. A tear rolled down his cheek as he thought of everything that could have been and of all the things he would want to redo. He could have been a better husband or father if he had been home more. He could have potentially prevented moments of pain and sadness that his wife endured over the years.

As he watched the two disappear into the jungle, he feared for their lives. *They're so young.* On second thought, he laughed to himself because Rusty was also old. But since he'd just woke up, he was still young in so many ways. The connection between Rusty and Alexa was strong. They endured together, fought for each other's lives from the beginning. It's not often in this world one finds a friend of this caliber. Rusty was earnest, thoughtful, courageous and sincere. He would make a good son-in-law. John wondered if it would ever happen. If he would even be alive . . . if they would still be alive at the end of the day.

He'd had to let them go without him. The truest of all from his military training was knowing his limits. He needed to rest and heal. As he thought of their potential encounters, he stood and chopped off a few large leaves, shredded them into a makeshift broom. Starting at the edge of the open area around Rusty's cabin, he cleared the prints and human disturbance over the course of the last few days. As he made his way back to the house, he cleaned the fire pit area by covering it with sand and dirt.

By the end of the day, the sky opened and drizzle covered the ground.

Taking this as a sign to rest, he decided to continue

reading Rusty's journal. He needed to read the last third. He kicked back his heels on a straw ottoman and admired Rusty's work. He was certainly a good jungle furniture maker. He laughed to himself for lack of a better term. Wiping the sweat from his brow, he read Rusty's recordings.

At the top of a plateau, I have discovered the southern half of the island, and I found an entryway into the ground. It seems to travel throughout the island. I first discovered this as I was traveling toward that strange churning noise. It seemed to radiate from this hole in the ground.

As I entered it, I was immediately intrigued; it was definitely made by a human. There were murals not too far in and stairs leading down, carved from stone. Old figurines, foreign in nature, sat on carved-out shelves and alcoves in the labyrinth of tunnels. I decided to construct my home on top of the tunnel I had found. There was also a river from the adjacent mountain that ran across the backside of the area where the tunnel resided. A good home it will be indeed.

John forwarded through the book and found another passage where the page was stained with blood.

I have found it—the source of the sound. He spoke to me originally in a dream a night back and told me the directions to him. I traveled the tunnels and ended up in a room surrounded by lava. It burned so hot and bright it was difficult to see or breathe. It led downward into a cooler, darker room where ornately dressed bones laid on its side facing a pool of a deep black liquid. These skeletal remains didn't look disgusting, rather it made me imagine that it looked aggravated. It looked as if the man was closing in on the pool but died before he reached it. Forever he would remain inches away from what he needed to survive. It was a strange thought, but I believed it to be true.

His voice came to me again as I looked down upon the skeleton. "Drink," it said with no movement of the skeleton's mouth.

Drink what? I certainly wasn't going to drink

that black liquid. I would maybe shine my boots with it, but it was not going into my mouth.

The voice spoke to me again as I attempted to leave the room, 'Drink it to help me pass on; I will give you a gift.'

I sat down beside his body and touched the liquid which was thick and shined as the light caught it. I rubbed it between my fingers and smelled it. It had a slightly metallic smell, and I would not imagine it wouldn't be too difficult to ingest.

I reached in and cupped my hands together. Dunking them into the small pool, I lifted my hands to my lips and drank. It tasted strange, but not horrible and exactly the way it smelled. I decided to document my encounter, and as I opened the first blank page, my fingers still covered in the liquid, touched the paper. I brought the light to my side and set it down, reaching for my quill when I realized what it was. With the light in view, the liquid's true color shined. It was red. It was blood.

A rustling in the leaves to the side of the house caught John's attention. He looked away from the journal.

Instinctively, he knew it couldn't mean anything good. He blew out the candle he was using to read, grabbed the knife, hopped off the back deck, and hid by the water. Watching closely as a figure appeared not far from his location, he waited.

John snuck behind the figure, covered its mouth with his left hand, and jammed the dagger in its back, puncturing its lung. He waited till the figure stopped squirming and placed it gently on the ground.

Four more beings entered the clearing from the western path. *No monkey warnings?*

He stepped back a few paces to control the angle between him and the four beings walking toward the house. Judging the distance to the entryway, he sank low to the ground and ducked behind a tree so they couldn't see him.

Suddenly, something screamed behind him. Turning quickly, a man jumped out at him. John tried to dodge the attack, but it was too late. The man's force thrust him backward. He hit his head on a tree and fell over. The four beings walking toward the cabin turned toward the scuffle. Screaming, they darted right for him. Surrounded,

John stood and lashed out.

John rolled off to one side and regained his footing. What were they? They resembled men but were short, dark, muscular, and their eyes glowed red.

One lunged in at him. He blocked his hand and kicked him in the head. The man dropped to the ground and screamed. The three others reached in all at once and wrestled John down to the ground. John thrashed and screamed at the beings, but they overtook him.

Just then, lightning struck down in the entrance of the path. Fierce and hard, the electricity tore at the ground for several seconds, glowing the earth beneath it. An outline of a man rose out of the bolt as it faded away.

"There is no reason to struggle. It is over now. Release him!" the outline commanded.

The beings let go of John, and he rose to his feet in shock at what just occurred. He stared at this outline, and it seemed somewhat familiar to him, yet he couldn't place it. This outline of a man stepped forward, his face illuminated in the moonlight. It was the man who stabbed him. John tore off to the side and tried to round the house and run down the path toward the broken bridge.

"There's no need to scurry!" the outline boomed out as the blackened beings tackled John to the ground.

John turned over to see the outline of the man bending toward him.

"What do you want from me?" John spat at the attacker.

"He wants you and I am here to bring you to him. Where are the other two?"

John shook his head and replied. "They left for the beach. Sorry you missed them. Who is 'he' and what's does he want with me?"

"He wants your life force. He wants your soul. It's time to go."

John felt himself being pulled upward. He was powerless to stop it. With all eyes on the sky, they watched as a light shown down from the clouds and illuminated Rusty's yard. Suddenly, a huge flash broke through the sky. Then everything vanished around him into nothingness.

CHAPTER 22

The stone staircase spiraled downward into blackness, and Alexa turned on her magic flashlight. She couldn't help but stifle a small laugh, even though the situation was dire.

Rusty shook his head and poked her. "Please try to remain serious."

"Sorry. I laugh when I'm nervous and scared, and when I use my powers of sorcery to produce light," she whispered back, watching as Rusty tightened his lips at her and shook his head with a grin.

"Let's go get your dad," Rusty urged her on as he slid his machete from his belt.

The two traveled deep into the tunnel as the glow from the flames began to illuminate from below. They crept to the first opening and peered through a hole in the wall of the forge.

The room glowed blood red as lava flows surfaced along the walls. Dark beings with mysterious red eyes hammered swords and other weapons and piled them in the center of the room.

Rusty pointed down the hall, suggesting they move past the forge and continue down.

Alexa agreed with a nod, and they silently stepped further down the spiral. Sweat ran down her back as rush of hot air shot through the tunnel.

The wall opened into a doorway where stairs protruded out and down and connected the room to the main stairwell. A man working on an anvil turned in their direction.

They froze, locking eyes on his position. Alexa's brow tensed as she stood frozen in silence.

The blackened being placed the blade he was working on into the blazing fire and wiped the sweat from his brow.

Rusty let out a sigh as quietly as possible. The blacksmith hadn't noticed them.

The doorway opened to a stone-walled room with a large throne in the middle. Flat marble floors shimmered with red from the holes in the ceiling that lead to the forge. The two stepped down the stairs and into the room quietly. Rusty looked up at the opening which lead to the forge. Through the hole, they could just make out a head of one of the blacksmiths, so they skirted to the side and stayed away from his angle.

An opening led out the back of the room, behind the throne, but was blocked with an iron door. They peered into the room through the bars in the door, and flickers of light bounced across the center of the room from candles nestled in large indents in the walls. The wax that dripped down the openings was incredibly thick, as if it was hundreds of years and thousands of candles that were needed to create such a flow. As opposed to the marble in the room they were standing in, this room had a black slate floor that had been meticulously laid. In the center, the slate rose upward and formed a pool.

On an adjacent platform lay a skeleton.

Alexa turned her head to the side looking at Rusty,

who gaped at the sight of the man. "What is it, Rusty. Is it *him*?" Alexa asked, breaking Rusty's gaze on the dead man.

"No, he's um . . ."

"Christopher . . . Alexa . . . help me," the skeleton muttered, drawing their attention back to him.

"Who are you?" Alexa questioned, before Rusty had a chance to compose his thoughts.

"Come closer," the skeleton spoke directly to their minds without making a sound.

§§§

Alexa immediately couldn't think clearly. The skeleton was in her head and everywhere at once. The pull he had erased all her emotions and replaced it with an incredible desire to come to him. She looked at Rusty and spoke to him with no words, suggesting they open the door and join the bones.

Rusty acted like he was in the same dream state and placed his hands on the handle to the iron door, but it was locked.

Just then footsteps behind them echoed across the room. The two silently slid behind the throne. A being appeared from the stairwell and entered the room. Blackened skin and reddish eyes glowed from under his hood, mirroring the forge's firelight. He was covered from head to toe in a robe made from tan jute. Two large candles hovered a few inches above his hands as he walked past the throne to the locked iron door.

Alexa and Rusty scooted around the throne as he passed by, looking around the chair to see what he was doing. The blackened being's left hand came out from the robe, palm upward. His right hand formed a symbol with his thumb and pinky finger touching, leaving his other three fingers together. He placed his right hand down on his left and a light glowed around him. It increased in intensity and the sound of the lock rang out.

The iron door creaked as it slid inward. Turning with outstretched arms, the candles hovered over his upward-facing palms.

"Now!" The voice spoke to Alexa. "Christopher, stay!" She replied within her mind, confirming the instruction. Alexa turned to Rusty and the machete floated to her hand. She shot into the room in a blur and slashed the being down. A swishing sound rang out in the room as the body fell. His robe dropped flat to the floor. The candles were still suspended in the air. Her killing blow disintegrated the being, leaving only black dust.

"Good work, my child." He smiled at Alexa and looked at Rusty. "Christopher, take the robe. Alexa, please sit."

§§§

Rusty walked into the room and shook out the robe. Black dust floated into the air as he put it on and adjusted the sleeves.

"Christopher, sit with me. Or perhaps I should call you Rusty Mechanic?" the voice laughed in both of their heads, as Rusty knelt beside the skeleton, next to Alexa. "Christopher, it has been far too long since we last spoke. By my calculations, it has been over a thousand years. We should make haste. Place your hand on me."

As Rusty's hand contacted the skeleton's femur, visible energy pulled from Rusty to the remains of the man. Alexa, still in her dream-like state, was unshaken as Rusty's world entered the corpse.

"I see now. I understand why it has been so long. Cretus has removed your memories of me to keep you away. Smart. Very smart." The voice of the skeleton turned his attention to the girl. "Let me explain to Alexa. I am Dragul, son of Jalon. I shall read you a passage from my father's hand so that you may understand."

The voice spoke to them both simultaneously as he recited a passage from The Testament of Jalon.

'"I have created two sons to watch over the lands. Two pure souls, Cretus and Dragul. Together, they will control the energy of the world and all that exists. Both constructed of pure light. I place my sons on opposite sides—the Island of Souls and the Heart Island. Apart, they can rule. Yet, together, they can unite. They are not perfect but that is their goal.'"

Dragul, now in skeleton form, continued speaking to them.

"My brother became jealous of my earthly wife. He has imprisoned me and killed her. But before my wife passed, a child was born. This infant, created of pure love, hidden from Cretus's sight, passed upon this gift to the world and the stars. The beginnings of a blood line were created, hidden from his view.

He bled me out into this pool, weakening me. He is trying to destroy me, but he could not, because I am distributed through my child. For centuries, he could not detect the blood of my wife because it had been diminished. Silver shined amongst the heavens, reflecting the essence of pure love once more—your necklace. He had found the lineage which orbited the planet just out of reach.

Alexa, you are the last descendant of my wife's blood.

Cretus has expelled his energy in our battle and continues to use it in search of you, Alexa.

Rusty, you are a part of me, and if Cretus receives your soul, he will take full form again. Cretus is confused and thinks John is connected, but he is not. I have limited ability from this state, but I could sway his direction.

The last major encounter left Rusty without memory, as Cretus has done in the past. Because of Cretus's frustrations in his quest for the bloodline, he threw you into the sea. He is not strong enough to kill you. He needs Alexa to rid us forever.

We will rise together and restore balance. Place my earthly bones in the pool now so I can take form once more."

Rusty and Alexa stood on opposite sides of the skeleton and leaned down to get a hold on Dragul. Gently, they lifted the skeleton and carefully inched their way toward the pool.

"Halt!" a voice roared and shot out a bolt of energy at Alexa. With a crack of blue light, she was thrown off the platform. A sickening snap of bones rang out as her body smashed against the wall. She fell to the ground and landed in a seated position. Blood covered the wall and oozed from her mouth.

Rusty dropped the skeleton of Dragul, shattering portions of the bones on the platform.

"It is my time, my friends," the voice echoed in the cavern. "I am Cretus. It will be all over soon."

Rusty ran to his love and supported her head and shielded her from the demi-god.

"Get John, you imbeciles," Cretus commanded, yelling toward the stairwell. There came a pitter patter of feet as one of the dark beings descended the stairs, unseen. Moments later, Bobby and three minions carried John, badly beaten and unconscious, into the room and placed him near Rusty and Alexa.

Alexa floated in and out of consciousness, barely hanging on to life. As a last hope, Rusty kissed her deeply, and she began to fade away, taking her with him once more. They both hovered in space, leaving their bodies behind for a moment.

"Rusty, I'm sorry I couldn't make it. I'm dying," she sobbed to him. "I wanted so desperately to free you, to be with you, but I failed you!"

"You didn't, my love," Rusty whispered to her. "You have given me hope in this endless life. I will save you. Please hold on."

A large bang in the room brought the two back. As Rusty broke the kiss from Alexa, he turned to see Lucky shoot through the door and take out one of the beings holding John. The other two beings chased Lucky as she raced across the room, dodging and weaving like the wind on four legs. Heading toward the pool, Lucky sprinted and was caught off guard by a blast of lightning from Cretus. Lucky hit the ground, instantly killed, and slid across the platform, pushing the skeleton into the pool and splashing in after him.

The pool now bubbled, and a faint glow appeared over it. A horrific sound of agony filled all ears in the room as the glow deepened in color from grey to crimson red. The magnitude of the screams brought everyone to their knees, including Cretus who couldn't maintain his hovering. The pool drained as a being emerged out from the glow.

"Bow before me, Cretus!" Dragul commanded with an earth-shocking presence. The force of his words shook the foundation of the cavern, dislodging rocks and collapsing tunnels.

"I refuse!" Cretus screeched as rage coursed through him, sending lightning across the room.

Dragul vanished into smoke and reappeared in front of Bobby in a flash.

"You fool! You have nearly killed us all!" Dragul roared as his pearlescent fangs grew and shined in the light. Dragul surged at Bobby's neck and sucked the life out of him. As Dragul rose again, blood dripped from his mouth and sizzled as drops hit the tiles. Wrinkled and flaccid, the shell of Bobby lay on the floor, dead.

Rusty watched in fear as Dragul hovered above the ground and regained strength. Looking down at his love, Alexa was silent and not moving. He called to her, but she didn't respond. He shook her and screamed her name, but she wouldn't wake. Frantically, Rusty scrambled over to the pool to gather some of the liquid for Alexa. He needed to save her. The pool was dry. All that was left was the lifeless body of Lucky.

The caverns rocked and crashed all around them as the roof of the cave system began to collapse. Rusty cried out, throwing himself at the edge of the platform. Lucky and Alexa were dead.

Rocks and lava erupted around Rusty as Cretus shook the top of the caverns. He stood and faced Dragul and pleaded, but the god shook his head and disappeared into smoke. Rusty's last hope had abandoned him.

He grabbed Alexa in his arms and attempted to evacuate. The ground shook as the gods met in battle. He lost his footing and fell. Rusty stood and grabbed Alexa once more. Step by step, as the walls collapsed around him, he trudged on, trembling.

A chunk of ceiling collapsed and smashed down the stairwell and into him. The force knocked him back into the room, bashing into his head. Blood drained from him as he lay on the floor holding Alexa. Rocks fell around their bodies, and one came crashing down on John's legs next to them.

The shock of the impact jolted John back into consciousness. He let out a horrific scream as he looked down at his mangled legs trapped under the large rock.

Rusty turned to him, crying and holding his love's lifeless body. The screams settled as John and Rusty's eyes met.

"I couldn't save her, John," Rusty cried out, rocking in the pile of rubble with Alexa in his arms.

John whimpered and reached out for his daughter, and Rusty carefully slid over to John, allowing him to embrace his dead child. Rusty fell over in grief as he placed the girl in John's arms. Both father and daughter lay on their backs facing the ceiling of the cave as it began to collapse.

Rusty kneeled over Alexa to hug John, but John put up a hand to block him.

"Rusty, the life is in you. It is in your blood. Don't infect me. I need to be with Janice."

Rusty backed off and sat and wiped his lips. Pulling away his hand away, his fingers were covered in blood.

"Save her." John pleaded and looked to his daughter.

Rusty placed his fingers on Alexa's lips, smearing them in his blood, and leaned in for a final kiss. Swirls of light surrounded them as their lips met in his dream. The floors and ceilings disappeared as he kissed her deeper. When the rush subsided, he looked around but she wasn't there with him.

"Alexa!"

No reply came.

She lay by his feet. Unmoving. It was too late. He broke from the kiss and was transported back to the cavern and back to John.

"It's okay, Rusty. I know you did everything you

could do." John whispered as the roof of the cavern gave way and killed them both.

§§§

Rusty woke on the beach far from the cavern. The sun blinded him for a moment, and he held his sandy hand over his forehead to shade his eyes from the blinding light. Sitting up, he struggled to let his eyes adjust, but tears blinded him. He realized he was looking out to where the cruise ship once rested.

Rusty's chest heaved as he convulsed in agony; he cried for John. A good, honest man, a loving father. He pleaded for Lucky, his faithful companion, full of energy and love. He wretched with devastation for the loss of Alexa, his love and the last in the blood line. His world was destroyed.

"Why are you crying, love?" A voice as gentle as a breeze came from behind him.

Rusty jerked his head to see Alexa and trotting behind her, Lucky.

Heart beating wildly, he heaved great sobs.

His life was about to begin.

ABOUT THE AUTHOR

As a crippled, illiterate orphan, Brian seemed destined to never be a high achiever, let alone an author. Not until his journal entries at the age of thirteen were his reveries first placed on paper. Vivid, wild, and untamed, his aptitude shined. His teachers read the entries in disbelief. It must have been plagiarism, they said. They didn't understand his need for the written word and further suppressed his imagination.

Crafting visions and scenes of a world of wonder helped Brian create and escape the traumas of his childhood.

Today he weaves his personal experiences and growth throughout the arcs of his characters. Brian intertwines the depth, struggles, and courage of humankind and playfully laces them with the lucid, unabashed dreams of a child.

Find out more information about Brian at:

http://facebook.com/brianneilroy

http://brianneilroy.com

Made in the USA
Middletown, DE
29 December 2016